THREATS

THREATS

AMELIA GRAY

FARRAR, STRAUS AND GIROUX   NEW YORK

Farrar, Straus and Giroux
18 West 18th Street, New York 10011

Library of Congress Cataloging-in-Publication Data
Gray, Amelia, 1982–
    Threats / Amelia Gray.—1st ed.
        p.   cm.
    ISBN 978-0-374-53307-6 (alk. paper)
    1. Missing persons—Fiction.   I. Title.

 PS3607.R387 T47 2012
 813'.6—dc23

                                    2011024952

Designed by Abby Kagan

www.fsgbooks.com

10 9 8 7 6 5 4 3 2

For my sister

THREATS

1.

THE TAPE ON THE PACKAGE was striped with waxed string. David dug his fingernails underneath the perimeter of the tape and clawed at it. He didn't want to go to the kitchen for a knife, and he spent an extra piece of time examining the entire package to find the loose end that could be pulled up. Inside the package was a Styrofoam carton, sealed with another kind of thick tape. A receipt was attached to the top of the lid, noting a cremation charge of $795, a box charge of $25, and a shipping charge of $20.95.

The package measured a few feet square. It was pockmarked with red stickers printed with the image of a broken wineglass. The return address was of a funeral home in town. David placed the package on the coffee table between Franny's cooking magazines and a stack of old newspapers. Some of the crosswords in the newspapers had been completed weeks earlier, perhaps months. Franny would read the news, and David would complete the crosswords. David took the newspapers into the basement and stacked them in a far corner.

2.

FRANNY had never faulted him his confusions. Once, a group
of squabbling jays stopped them on a walk. Two of the birds
were circling each other, ducking and weaving, thrusting beak
to wing, falling back. The group around that central pair collec-
tively made a noise like rushing water. They spread their blue
wings. It looked like someone had dropped a scarf on the ground.
They moved in a unified line around the fighters in the center.

She took his hand. "You're in the road," she said.

He knew he had found a good woman in Franny. After only
a few months of movie dates, they announced their engagement. The two of them took David's father out to dinner and
told him as the main course arrived. David's father thought
about how tall Franny was, how much taller she was than his
son. Even with the two of them sitting across the table from
him, he could see the fine, straight lines of Franny's spine
holding her higher than his poor thirty-year-old son, balding
young, who scrabbled after a piece of meat with one side of his
fork. Franny seemed stronger and older and smarter than his
boy. She used her butter knife to push the errant cube of steak

onto David's probing fork without breaking eye contact with David's father. *Still*, David's father thought, *marry a straight spine and she'll grow into a walking stick.*

David's regular patients asked the most questions. There were his childhood friends, Samson and the other one, the one whose name David could never remember even when he held the man's file, a file containing a near lifetime of dental history, on his lap. David kept in contact with his old friends over time because they came in yearly for checkups. They usually spoke of the small success and general failure of local sports. The hygienists were the ones who had let the engagement news slip, and then David was cajoled into producing a picture of his future bride, and then everyone asked about her grip strength and cooking skill, and if she could help them move a dinner table to a third-floor apartment.

The questions they asked were forward but mostly not impolite. One of his patients who worked in the art department at the local community college asked if Franny could stand for his life-drawing class, speculating that her anatomy would lend itself to easier visual interpretation.

"She's massive," said an uncle on his father's side, who came in from the country every few years for his teeth and had received an e-mail from the hygienists that included an image attachment. "I mean that kindly," he said, insisting it over the sound of applied suction.

David knew that his family and his patients were only trying to piece together the physical mystery of Franny. The truth was that he had always felt he was an average-size man until he met her and realized how small he truly was. He appreciated the perspective.

3.

FRANNY HAD RUN AWAY from home as a teenager and ridden the bus alone. David asked what made her do that, and she said there was nothing else going on. She remembered the time fondly. In order to buy the tickets, she spent her paychecks from working at a food court shake shop at the mall. She took a bus to visit a town with a coal-mine fire that would slowly burn striated fault lines for the next hundred years. The blaze had evacuated the area a decade before. Franny walked around while eating a cheeseburger from the bus terminal café. She lay on a bare patch of dirt at a school playground in the middle of the Pennsylvania winter and felt warm. A vent in the earth released a sour smell. The heat from the vent steamed against the falling snow, turning it to a drizzle before it hit the ground.

Though she never touched tobacco as an adult, teenage Franny would pluck cigarette butts from the kitty litter trays by the bus terminal door and smoke the dregs. One of the other passengers might witness this act and stroll over to offer the girl a cigarette from his pack, but she would refuse. She figured a whole cigarette would make her sick. Often, the cigarettes she found carried lipstick marks, like blushing thumbprints, and Franny would light up and imagine the kind of woman who applied lipstick to make the trip between Ohio and Michigan.

The filters she examined were ivory-colored and darkened in a spectrum that revealed the pull of the previous user. She could find plenty of near-new smokes in an ashtray at any given bus stop owing to people running to make their connection. She smiled when she thought of those years but admitted that it was a true miracle that she did not contract oral thrush. It seemed to David as if she could leave at any moment. She would get that look in her eye.

4.

HE KNEW FRANNY had been behind the house. She wore a scarf colored red like the berries that grew back there. Her feet were bare and her ankles were slick with fluid. "Something has happened," Franny said.

She was standing at the bottom of the stairs. She held the rail and tipped her head back to look at her husband. They held the same rail. "You've been tromping berries," he said.

"It's blood." She held the stair's rail and vomited down the front of her dress. "Could you call for help?" she asked, wiping her mouth with her fingers.

"Of course," he said. He commanded his body to find a telephone and determine its use. "What's the problem?"

"God, damn it," she said.

"What did you do?" he asked. "What happened?"

"Could you call the fire department?" She sat on the stairs and leaned against the wall with her back to him. He came down and sat next to her. He touched her cold face with his hands. "You don't need to call anyone," she said. "Forget about it. I love you."

"What did you get into?"

She tipped her head to the side and back, squinting at him or resting against the wall. "That's your problem," she said.

They were quiet for a long time. He listened to her breathing so closely that he forgot to breathe, himself. He gasped for air. He prodded at her with his elbow. "Doc," he said. "You gotta understand."

She laughed once.

David sat next to his wife for three days. They leaned against each other and created a powerful odor. In that way, it was like growing old together.

5.

DAVID decided that the police must have been tipped off by a neighbor who had wandered in a few days before.

"How long have you been here?" one officer asked.

"I'm not sure," David said. He was wrapped in a blanket. A firefighter was trying to strap an oxygen mask onto his face. "I'm sorry, I'm disoriented. I think there's enough oxygen."

"Not in your world," the firefighter said. David noticed that the firefighter was a woman. He felt the world shifting to the point where he was wearing her uniform. His straw-blond hair, which was hers, was pulled back into a ponytail. He had never experienced a ponytail. It felt as if his head was weighted from behind. The weight terminated at a single point, which gave him the sense that there was an opening back there that might allow fluids to escape. His lips felt thin, and he watched her, as him, sitting on the stair. His face had sunk around its bones like soft earth, and the oxygen mask protected his mouth like a clear carapace sheltering his organs.

David wasn't sure how to tell her what needed to be said. He needed to be brave and gather his emotions for the sake of professionalism. It wasn't the first time he had called upon this professional bravery, though it always felt like the first time and in fact currently felt like the very first time. "Your wife is dead," he said.

The firefighter swallowed something. She looked as helpless there as a fifty-year-old man, and David felt pity. He reached toward his pocket for a tissue before realizing that he was wearing a firefighter's uniform and there were no pockets, only reflective strips that would glint against traffic lights and fires.

"I'm so sorry," he said.

She held her hands on the oxygen mask as if it were an extension of her face.

"We're going to have to ask you a few questions," David said.

She shook her head. "I can't," she said. Her voice was muffled by the mask. "I don't understand. What happened?"

"That's normal," David said. "What you're feeling is normal." He could see her eyes inside his, even as he occupied her body. It felt warm in the retardant uniform. He took on her memories. He felt a strong desire to sit with her in a bathtub and wash her shoulders. He clapped a gloved hand on her pale, cold thigh, which was half covered by David's filthiest robe, a green-and-black flannel that always looked as if it had been crammed into the space between the water heater and the wall.

David and the firefighter crouched in the stairwell. He felt as if he was looking down from the position of an angel who could not get much vertical distance over the scene. He turned awkwardly in the bulky retardant suit to observe the base of the stairs. It was caked with the fluid and gunk sloughed from the mess of a living body and a dying one. His pajama pants rested in a filthy heap below.

He looked to the firefighter occupying his body and saw that her left foot had retained its slipper, but the other foot was bare. The second slipper was forgotten at the base of the stairs. The firefighter was still swaddled by the blanket. The smell rising from the stairwell and steaming from her was an embarrassment of childhood odor. It made David dizzy to experience it, and he tried to focus on the thin face blurred behind the oxygen mask.

"I'm sorry," she said. She was crying. David had never seen such emotion from a public servant, other than the time a post office clerk was informed of his daughter's death via telephone in the midst of a Christmas rush, and now he was observing it happening in his own body. He had seen the post office clerk take the phone call and put his head in his hands, sobbing, resting his elbows on an electronic scale. David had been there to mail a package of documents to his mother's lawyer, but he was touched by the display and later sent flowers to the post office. He didn't know the clerk's name and addressed the lilies to the office in general. It seemed like the right thing to do from a taxpayer perspective.

The firefighter clutched the blue blanket and took shallow breaths. She tried to touch her face again and felt the oxygen mask and moved it out of the way. David reached his glove out to touch her arm, then removed the glove and touched her with his bare hand. He moved the mask back over her face.

"Get it all out," he said. "Would you like to talk about what happened?"

The firefighter scrubbed at her face and mouth. "I can't talk about it," she said. "I'm so confused."

David felt like a dog peering dumbly into the darkest moment of his owner's life. "That's normal," he said.

He noticed a pain in his arm and saw that he was taking fluids intravenously. He was inside the dimensions of his own body again. The oxygen mask lined his face and the calming smoothness made his eyelids heavy. And there was Franny, resembling a piece of modern furniture under the police tarp. Her body had vacated its bowels beside him at some point in their time together on the stair. He cherished the life implied by that action, the odor of a living thing beside him, pulsing bacterial life that had once been harbored by her body, not unlike a child, ejected now into the dimming light, bacteria feeding on itself and fading. He wondered if a florist might deliver lilies to the stairwell. Franny's body had grown stiff and then soft again beside him on the stair, and by then it must have been as pliable as a wax figure. In the police business of securing the area, she was forgotten on the floor. A paramedic stepped over her. *Sweet Franny*, David thought.

6.

DAVID WAS FAMILIAR WITH DECAY. When his father died, the house's basement was the unspoken casualty. His father used to head down there even when he had trouble walking, holding on to the banister and taking breaks between steps, breathing heavily, examining imperfections in the wall. When he reemerged, he might say, "Underfoot and out of mind," but he would always go back. David heard his father in the basement almost every evening in those last days. It sounded like he was riffling through boxes and tapping nails into boards.

After the man's death, the basement had become submerged in neglect. What had once been a guest bedroom, bathroom, den, workshop, and concrete-floored storage area became a single entity of waste. Dust drifted from the unscrubbed vents and made a soft layer over the tools in the workroom. The guest bedroom clogged with rot. The water in the bathroom's toilet dried and created a mineral line on the ceramic. A bird built its nest on the cracked basement window, and twigs scattered onto the floor inside. With no other source of fresh air, mold populated the damp walls. Pipes grew an ecology of rust. A single green shoot emerged from the bathroom sink's drain. The walls seemed fuzzed. Cardboard softened in the damp. A pile of leaves in the guest bedroom resembled a squirrel drey. The closet in the bedroom held coats made lighter by moths. One member of a row of canned peaches on the wall in the storage area had burst, leaking fluid down the wall, attracting ants, which attracted lizards, which attracted a cat, who scratched through a basement screen and left the squirming reptilian tails of its prey behind. The cat vacated before David found any of the damage, but it left its ammonia-rich urine on a stack of cookbooks in the corner of the storage room. He covered the books with more cookbooks, which he had moved down from the kitchen because he didn't want to see them anymore. The flood from a water heater explosion only served to unify everything as a solid, decaying layer.

A highlight of the basement collection was an inversion table, a symbol of the last victory of David's mother. In his middle age, David's father bought the table. It looked like an ironing board split in half and propped on four sturdy legs. He would strap his ankles into the supports at the base, then release a lever and push back, turning himself upside down on a horizontal axis at waist level, allowing him to hang by his ankles, his head and arms swinging between the supports. The purpose was spinal decompression. As a child, David would come downstairs in the morning to find his father inverted in the center of the living room, craning his neck to watch television. "Gravity," his father would say. "Take a cue from the planets."

David's mother hated the device and refused to dust it. Before she went away, she made a daily case for its move to the basement, where it would be out of sight and less of a general hazard. David's father tried to sell the table in order to help pay the bills after she left. Finally he moved it, and it remained, almost hidden under a carload of old road atlases, in the basement.

David went down and surveyed the scene a week after his father's funeral. He saw the lizard tails and the evidence of sagging rot and then closed the door behind him on the way out. He couldn't bear to gather what he had been looking for, the old organized dental files and contacts that had once been a proof of his value and were becoming the hallmark of his personal depreciation. He liked to look at them in the way that similarly sentimental people liked to look at their own baby pictures and the baby pictures of their parents. When he closed the door to the basement behind him, an old, dry fountain pen fell from over the door frame and rolled into the hallway.

7

IT WAS EASY to stand in line at the post office. The action required walking for thirty minutes beside the road, but David walked. Three buses passed him. It was a comfort to know that every footstep was possible. Earlier, he had let workers into his house. They arrived with proof of license and an order to clean the stairs. He wasn't sure who had sent them, but his own presence in the house while they were there made him feel uneasy.

The post office was a low brick building. The handrails that flanked it looked as if they'd been painted blue a thousand years before. Standing beside them meant becoming intimately linked to a moment in history.

Inside, individuals entered their personal information onto slips of paper. A woman smiled at David and pointed at a change-of-address form in front of him. He passed it to her and she accepted it with a slight, half-bowing nod. Everything seemed possible at the post office. The customers brought canisters and tubes and small cubes to the counter, and the men and women behind the counter accepted these objects and affixed them with stamps and stickers indicating their destination and contents, and at that moment they were in America, everyone in that room was in a city in Ohio in a country called America and the packages were in America and they were all a part of that.

David looked for the postal clerk who had wept but could not find him. He thought about how each of the postal clerks had likely wept at some point in time, though he had not witnessed it. When it was his turn at the counter, he produced a piece of paper that he had found in his mailbox.

The clerk accepted and examined the page. "You've got to be checking your mail every day," he said.

David didn't very much like the idea of speaking, but the man seemed kind in an unsmiling way. "I'm sorry," David said. "Things got out of hand."

The man tapped the card once on the counter and began to enter David's information into his computer. "I'll need some identification," he said. David saw flashes of lateral incisor. He handed over his driver's license.

"You can always come down here and stop your mail," the man said. "We'll hang on to it for you."

"Thank you."

"No thanks necessary, sir. It's the duty of the United States Postal Service." He tapped David's license on the counter again and slid it across the table. "I'll fetch your mail."

He went into the back room and returned with a bundle of junk and bills. A card banded to it bore David's name. David accepted the gift and felt that it would be possible to survive. It was good to be out of the house.

8.

WHEN HE RETURNED HOME, the workers were still there. They were pulling up carpet on the stairs. They had seemed kind enough when he let them in before, but after he left, they put on hazmat suits and masks and stood on the stairwell, where he had recently spent a concentrated span of time. It had been enough trouble to get around them on the way up the stairs, and David didn't want to do it again. He sat in the bedroom and smelled its occupied smell. He imagined that the comforter was packed with particles of skin, and stretching out on it made him feel cradled in a hand. He rolled to his side, opened the compartment on the back of the digital clock, and ticked out the battery with his fingernail.

The workers were listening to classic rock from a portable radio. David heard one of them singing along. The music sounded filtered or reversed. Still, it felt good to have some activity in the house. He remembered the sound of his mother announcing breakfast.

He didn't remember calling the workers, but he did remember letting them into the house. He was glad they were there.

It was hard to leave the bedroom. He heard them calling out to one another over their machines in the stairwell. Their voices came to his ears as a comforting hum. David moved to the floor and sat with his back to the bed.

Eventually they came to speak to him. One of them helped him up and brought him to the stairwell, where he saw that their work was done. The human waste was gone, as was the carpeting. They had cut a clean line in the carpet at the top of the stairs and ripped it all out, removing nails, sanding down what remained. The walls and wood had been cleaned with a solvent. The men had taken the hoods off their hazmat suits, and their faces were ruddy and flushed, suggesting a fine day of accomplishment. He couldn't understand what they were saying behind all the buzzing, but they seemed pleasant and kind to him, and he nodded. It did register to him that they were speaking in English, but they were saying things he couldn't follow. One of the men reached out with a gloved hand. David felt confused. He heard a ukulele. The men looked at one another. They seemed very kind.

When they didn't leave, it occurred to him that they might require some form of payment. He found a set of silverware in a velvet box and gave it to them, smiling. He bowed slightly, the way the woman in the post office had bowed, a gesture of respect.

The men left through the front door. David had been holding the digital clock battery between his cheek and his right maxillary second molar. Once they were gone, he ejected it into his hand. He observed it, whole and unconcealed, with no small amount of satisfaction.

9.

FRANNY had been an aesthetician, specializing in pore extraction and deep chemical peels. She talked infrequently about her job, becoming vague about the details like she was afraid to give away too much. "It's more complicated than that," she would say, and change the subject without elaborating.

About a week after the workers took out the carpet on the stairs, five women from the salon came by and offered to cut David's hair. They wore matching tank tops and salon aprons and arrived unannounced. One of them laid a plastic sheet on the kitchen floor and put a chair from the dining room in the center of it. They had brought clippers and products.

"We can do something about this salt and pepper," said one, yanking on a fistful of hair. "Update the look a little?"

David felt the paper band stretched around his neck like a cleric's collar. He thought of ways to politely refuse.

"Let's keep foils out of it," said another girl, and David realized that the first girl hadn't been talking to him before, despite looking at him and speaking to him, and that this was a thing that would continue to happen.

"It's nice of you all to do this," David said. "Franny always said you were so generous." She had never said such a thing about anyone, but he felt it was important to get her involved. A young woman sat on the floor and painted his toenails with clear polish.

"Frances always bugged us to come here and cut his hair," one of the girls said, brushing clippings from his shoulders. "We figured we ought to. She didn't want to do it herself and she said it was getting pretty bad, since he never leaves the house."

"Even up the ears," said another.

"I do leave the house."

"Aileen said."

Franny had one close friend while she was alive, a coworker. Aileen was a nice woman but strange, and she held what David felt was an excessive interest in the salon.

"These toes," said the one on the floor.

"She said I never leave the house?"

"I don't like this spot on his neck."

Another leaned in and began plucking the hair between his eyebrows. "Frances said he likes things to be a certain way."

"Who doesn't like things to be a certain way?"

They looked at one another and shrugged, a wave of shifting tank top straps.

"She said that a man can make himself busy around his home," one said.

"Frances said that," said another.

"She was so beautiful," added another.

"Too busy," said the first.

"Thank you," he said, and "I am," and "It's true," in an order that made the girls briefly cease their instrument movement and look at him with small smiles. One of them scratched her belly with the side of her shears, wincing in pleasure. "We all like things to be a certain way," she said.

"He's been through a lot lately," said another, tugging the first girl's shirt down to cover her midriff.

One of the girls said nothing the whole time, but instead hummed a song that was familiar to David. He thought of his mother cutting his hair while he sat on a wooden chair wedged into the bathtub.

The girl who had been scratching her belly advanced on David with floss strung between her fingers. "Open up," she said cheerfully, and David obligingly leaned back and opened his mouth. The girl plunged her small hands inside and tucked the floss around his teeth. He heard the popping noise of glutinous bits emerging between his second and third molars. The girl rotated her fingers and dipped the floss between his teeth more expertly than the hygienists David had known. As part of his interview process at the dental office, he had set it up so that they would floss him. He could get a better sense of how they handled floss and teeth and various pressure. He could tell a set of hands fumbling with nervousness from a pair that had been undereducated or were simply clumsy, pressing farther when they caught gingival sulcus, causing blood to well up from David's taut gums. With the woman from the salon, he felt his gums plucked and loved.

"You're good," he said, running his tongue over his teeth when she removed her hands. There was no slick of blood on the floss.

She unwrapped the string from her fingers and dropped it in the garbage pail. "I used to have to floss my brother," she said, patting his knee.

"We figured a man who didn't leave the house before would really never leave now," said the one on the floor. "After everything happened."

When they were done, the women removed the cape and paper collar and gave him a handheld mirror to look at. They packed their scissors and products into black canvas bags and folded the plastic tarp with his hair inside. One tucked the chair back under the table. They hugged him one by one, and he gave them each a book that he picked from his library. This transaction occurred by the door. One of the girls reached for the doorknob and drew her hand back, wincing. "Damn shock," she said.

"Winter," said another.

The girls waved as their car pulled out of the driveway. David waved back and thought again about the hygienists he had known. There was one he had liked while he was in dental school who made him quiz her when she studied for her tests. Another, who must have been that girl's friend, put her hand on David's thigh at a party and asked if he knew of any eligible bachelors in school. They made him nervous, these girls. The ones he hired at his office were all intelligent and professional and good with teeth. They were all girls to him, fresh-faced, out of trade school at twenty, worrying about how their underage bridesmaids might drink at their weddings.

He was by no means attracted to the girls, who, with their unmarked faces, shared more features with ambulatory fetuses than with women. Franny teased him anyway, asking him where he had been when he arrived late, noting how comfortable his reclining examination-room chairs were, speculating on the smell of bergamot on his body, a scent David wouldn't be able to identify even if he knew what it meant. It sounded like a flower. Still, Franny would tease him as he sat at the table or lay down in bed, naming scents, claiming to smell lavender or brown sugar, touching his hand at dinner and bringing it to her face, recognition narrowing her eyes. Her scent changed when she began working at the salon, but, she said, that was different.

10.

WHEN THE OFFICERS ARRIVED at his front door, David found himself mentally unable to touch the doorknob.

"I'm sorry," he said. "I never use this door."

"Is there a problem?" one of the officers asked from the other side.

The door's lock was a mystery. Its silver dead bolt gleamed, barely visible through the crack in the jamb. David wondered if the bolt was electrified and immediately became convinced that it was. If the bolt itself was laced with energy, how much would travel through the actuator? How much force would have to be employed to push the engaged device horizontally through the jamb? At that moment, was he safe? David did not feel safe.

One of the men outside straddled a bush and knocked on the window. The glass rattled in the frame and the frame strained on its tracks. David urinated silently down his left leg. He shifted sideways from the window, covering his thigh with his hand. "I'm sorry," he called out.

"We want to ask you some questions," the officer said. "Please, David. Open the door."

There were so many ways anyone could learn his name. David thought of how easy it would be to take a piece of his mail from the mailbox.

He pressed his cheek to the doorjamb. Air whistled out or in. "How did you know?" he asked. His slipper was wet, his leg, his hand. He held his breath to listen.

"We want to talk to you," said the officer at the window. "What are you doing?"

David removed his pants and underwear and slippers and slid them into a far corner. The scent of urine coated both hands. "I'm sorry," he said. He sat on the floor by the window. "I've had a difficult day."

From his spot, he could see the officer on the front porch as well as the one standing at the window. The lawn was graded so that David and the officer were at eye level, though David was seated and the officer stood. "You have removed your pants," the officer said. The radio on his shoulder buzzed with activity.

David pointed. "They're over there."

"The man urinated," the officer at the window, whose name badge read CHICO, said to the officer on the porch. The window was an old single-pane variety, which made it easier to talk and listen.

David sat cross-legged on the floor. "I'm sorry, Officer Chico."

"We don't require an apology," said Chico. He was an older man, maybe ten years older than David, but he possessed an energy in his eyes that David did not. "You are a man in your own home. You have the freedom to act within the confines of the law."

"That's a refreshing opinion from a member of law enforcement."

Chico turned down the volume control on his radio. "Also, I am a detective."

"You sound like a smart guy," said the man on the porch.

"Pay no mind to my partner," said Chico. "Justice holds the progressive close to her breast. Anyway, we see it all the time."

David closed his eyes. The wood floor felt smooth on his nakedness. "Her heart may bleed," he said, "but the scales are forged with hands wrought heavy by tradition."

"Urine, I mean," said Chico. "How are you feeling?"

"I'm confused all day," said David.

"That's understandable. Do your friends come by? Family members?"

"I got a haircut."

"Give me a break," said Chico's partner.

The detective pulled a notepad from his back pocket. "Could you give us the names of some people we could contact?"

David knew he would enjoy very much the feeling of a woman placing her palms on his face. "Someone altered my clocks," he said.

"We don't want to alter your clocks, sir."

"I'm concerned."

"Could you look at me?"

Chico was bundled in police-issue winter gear, which included a heavy coat, his badge pinned to the lapel. "Neither myself nor Officer Riley over there is going to alter your clocks," he said.

"Maybe clean 'em," Riley said.

"That's not as helpful as you might assume, Officer Riley,"

said Chico, keeping eye contact with David. "Sir, please let us in. We do have the power to make this unpleasant."

David hooked his fingers under the window's sash. "It has already been unpleasant," he said. He pulled with no luck, then squatted and pushed up. The sash groaned and lifted, and he felt cool air against his face and lower body. His skin felt moist and young as he leaned close to Chico's face. "I am concerned that the dead bolt is electrified," he said.

11.

THE MEN seemed exceptionally kind, considering that one had crawled through the window. David apologized to them for the trouble, and they apologized for interrupting him. Officer Riley found a blanket and a small cardboard box in the trunk of the squad car. He tossed the blanket to David and deposited David's wet clothes in the cardboard box. He left the box at the base of the stairs.

Riley led the way to the kitchen and began going to some trouble to find instant coffee and mugs. He boiled water in a pot someone had left on the stove. Chico walked the perimeter of the room, his arms crossed.

David stood in the doorway and watched them both. He felt comfortable and warm, wrapped in the police blanket from the waist down. He imagined that if his house was on fire, he would want to be wrapped in that same blanket while standing on the street. The feeling of being swaddled as an adult was foreign and tender.

"The city has no shortage of blankets," David said. "Have they considered opening a Salvation Army?"

Chico removed his gloves and raised one hand toward Riley. "You know, that's a fine idea," he said to David.

The men stood, listening to the sound of the hissing range as it heated the water. "The dead bolt was not electrified," David said. "I was glad to learn that was the case."

"As were we," said Chico. "Why would it have been?"

"I feel swaddled."

"Understandable."

Riley took the pot of boiling water from the stove and filled the cups. The instant grounds soaked to become an approximation of coffee as the officer carried the remaining water to the sink.

"You'll bust the pipes," David said.

Riley looked at him. He turned to put the pot back on the stove.

"There are some numbers on the friends," David said. "For my fridge."

"Your feelings are understandable," Chico said.

Watching as Riley opened his notebook and examined the numbers on the fridge, David leaned in toward Chico. "I don't trust that man," he said.

"Do you trust me?"

David frowned.

"I am trying to find out what happened to your wife," Chico said. "I am going to be coming back to talk to you over the next few days. I want you to be ready for that. We're going to come back and talk to you. I don't want you to be alarmed, David. Take your head out of your hands and look at me. I don't want you to be alarmed. What happened to your wife has become a question for members of local and state law enforcement."

"These are numbers for hospitals," Riley said. "There's a plumber, a salon. Do you have any personal contacts?"

"I certainly don't want you to be alarmed," Chico said, "but I'm going to ask a lot of questions and not provide a lot of answers. I hope you appreciate my candor and relative honesty at this time."

"Relative candor."

"And honesty. Right."

David swirled his coffee. "I believe there is glass in this," he said.

Chico lowered his cup. "What inspires that concern, David?"

"The glass broke. I worry it found its way in."

"When did this happen?"

David pictured the broken glass. They had eaten meatloaf afterward. It must have been winter. Franny sat at the table, drinking from the bottle of wine. She had the ability to look at him as if she was an animal peering in through a window. "I had much more hair at the time," David said.

"Was this a long while ago?"

The ring on her finger tapped against the bottle when she raised it.

"David, when did you break the glass?"

"The glass broke yesterday." He could not remember the time.

"Was Franny there?"

"Her hair was longer." He knew enough to know that hair falls out in autumn, when it reaches the end of its follicle cycle. Two willing partners could make a home with the shedding. It had always seemed unlikely to David, but now he seriously considered living in a comfortable room lined with the product of years of naturally fallen hair.

"It could not have been yesterday, then."

"We had enough hair between us for a home," he said. "Franny and myself."

"David, it wasn't yesterday."

"Why not?"

Chico opened his mouth. Inside his mouth was a nest, and inside the nest there were three blue pills huddled up against one another like eggs. David leaned close to examine the pills. They jostled, alive on the man's tongue. Saliva dampened the sides of the nest. His mouth made a warm incubator. David could not determine the nest's composition. It looked like sharded toothpicks at first, but closer examination yielded a softer substance, such as a slivered reed wound around itself. The pills were precisely the size of those in the packet that Franny had kept by the toilet for years, exactly the same but for the fact that the pills on Chico's tongue maintained their own individual life.

"I see," said David.

When Chico exhaled, one of the pills rolled to the lower edge of the nest, looking like it might fall to the floor between them.

"Listen," David said, closing his eyes. "You should come back another day. I hope you would do me the honor of leaving now and returning another day for pleasant conversation. I will receive you at some time in the future. At the moment, you see, I'm not feeling well. I have been through a lot. I'm sure you understand."

He remained there with his eyes closed until the men left. Once they were gone, he rubbed his forehead, his eyes. He brought the water to a second boil and poured it down the sink.

12.

WHEN DAVID LEFT the dental practice, Franny experienced a natural adjustment period. Anyone would do the same, David reasoned. There was a financial arrangement to consider, as they began to rely on Franny's income from the salon. She started bringing home liter bottles of shampoo. Meanwhile, he settled comfortably back into his habits from dental school. He mixed chicory in his coffee and avoided using the heater.

One day while Franny was away, he took out all the forgotten food in the freezer. There were bricks of ground beef fuzzed over with frost, pints of old ice cream with one hard spoonful remaining. There were stale potpies, which David used to eat when nobody else was home, and four tubes of concentrated apple juice from years ago, when they had thought of throwing a party but decided against it.

He put a potpie in the oven and the beef in the sink. He let the ice cream thaw for an hour and drank the watery substance that remained. He mixed three pitchers of apple juice and lined them up in the fridge. He didn't have a fourth pitcher so he mixed the remaining juice in an old vase. He drank apple juice and ate the potpie, which had leached in the flavors of the freezer and tasted like plastic and wet paper. He thought about how the potpie was a product of its environment.

When Franny came home, she found the freezer-burned meatloaf next to a potpie that was old enough to attend middle school. Her mother's vase was full of juice in the center of the table. The sight of the vase reminded her of the woman her mother had been, the kind of woman who cleaned a vase with a moistened cotton swab in the event that someday, if someone felt the urge to drink juice out of it, they could pursue that urge. Franny sat down to eat with her husband.

13.

FRANNY NEVER CAME TO DAVID in dreams, and he respected her for that. He had heard of ghosts that moved through empty houses, opening cabinets or moaning in the hallway. There was the variety of ghost that sat at the foot of the bed and smiled, but when you reached toward it, you found only the sheets twisted around your legs and the darkness of the room beyond. Ghosts might leave footprints on a porch or follow you down a crowded street, staying just far enough behind and ducking into an alley every time you turned around. There was the kind of ghost who would fill a room with her scent. There were ghosts that traveled in a collective of ghosts, making a competition of it, ticking points off their list as they haunted the darker hallways of historical buildings.

There were ghosts that disguised themselves as glowing orbs in photographs, in such a way that some people would claim they were simple tricks of the light, overexposure of the camera or imperfections in the lens, while others would doubt the trick and believe. The ghosts, which could have appeared in any shape, orblike or otherwise, had the power to trick the living while still making their presence known. All ghosts found this to be very funny.

Some ghosts were mute, and other ghosts murmured to keep themselves company. Some had the power to throw chains against walls, but they were ghost chains and behaved differently from chains one might find wrapped in a coil at a hardware store. There was sound without weight, because the ghosts rarely had the power to lift more than the individual hairs on a pair of arms. It was a frustration to the ghosts, many of whom had spent long lives lifting things. Ghosts tended to express their frustration by causing trouble. A few dug around in trash cans. They pulled out cotton swabs and left them scattered around the room. When the victim entered, he worried that things were not as they seemed.

If Franny was out there somewhere, frustrated, she made no sign. She was the type to employ the silent treatment. He remembered her frowning past him, sitting alone on the couch with one of her magazines, then taking the magazine and heading out back.

She always seemed to end up in the woods behind the house when she was upset. He followed her out there once and found her standing by the stream on the far side of the farmer's fence. The stream was dry most of the year or covered in snow or leaves from the ash trees or ice, forming a thin line of flowing water when it warmed up enough for the snow to melt. When she saw he had followed her, Franny turned around and went back inside, and there was no dinner later. David toasted a piece of bread.

After that, he let her stay in the woods as long as she wished. She would go out unannounced and stay all day, returning hours later with webs in her hair.

14.

IT HAD BEEN A CLOUDLESS SPRING DAY near
the end of Chico's first month as an officer, forty years before.
He and his new partner got the call to head to an old motel.
The place was boarded up and vacant but still had its signs up
advertising color TV and a reduced rate, the rooms wrapped
around a near-empty parking lot. The locks on the doors had
been bashed away, and most rooms were home to off-book ten-
ants favoring methamphetamines over their off-book kids, who
cried bitterly and scrubbed their faces. The city had organized
most of the resources required for a sting operation on the place
but hadn't yet collected enough money for a battering ram.

The call came in concurrently with an ambulance call for
a drowning. No residents came out to greet the siren. The noise
set off wails from two or three children who were heard but not
seen in the recesses of the motel. Their noise made it seem as
if the building itself was crying, the sound released from multiple points.

"Assholes," said the older officer, knocking on the last door
and then kicking it with some affection using the side of his

boot. The ambulance arrived as Chico and his partner made the rounds. The paramedics either had been given more information or knew by instinct, and they took their gear to the pool.

The pool, long since drained, had found a second life dedicated to collecting rain and mosquitoes. A foot of green water shone and stank at the bottom, dotted with leaves and rust, which served to highlight the white blemish of a naked child floating facedown. One of the paramedics waded in with a stabilizing board smaller than any Chico had seen before. He turned the child's body, secured it to the board, and lifted it up in his arms. Chico smelled burning plastic and asphalt. His kit belt was heavy around his waist. Each night that month, he took the belt off and rubbed a balm into the rashed skin.

The paramedic carried the board to the shallow end, where his partner was waiting. The child looked to be a toddler, a little girl, two or three years old. Her stomach was distended and her eyes were mottled with sludge. One of the girl's arms was shrunken, which gave it the appearance of being held protectively close. Her body was naked, save for a bulbous white cloth diaper. Chico watched the paramedics swab the child's face. He thought he saw some slight movement in the body and stopped walking to confirm that there was none. When he walked closer, he saw the twitch again. He was sure of it. The paramedics were packing up their supplies, kneeling next to the child.

"You checked the pulse," Chico said.

The bigger paramedic put his hand on his chest and looked back at him. "You scared me," he said.

"I want to make sure we follow protocol."

"Jesus, you scared me. I thought you were back there by the wall and then you came up behind me and scared the word out of me. My goodness." He touched the edge of the board. "This one's gone," he said.

"You checked her pulse, though." He came closer, standing nearly overhead. He lifted his hand to block the sun from the child's closed eyes. "You know what they say about protocol."

The paramedic squinted at him. "What do they say?"

Chico understood that it seemed impossible for the child to be alive, but holding his hand over the sun seemed to shift the girl's features, as if a flutter of a pulse could be coaxed out with the right lighting conditions. He held up another hand and shaded the child's entire face. "It's there," Chico said, both hands stretched high. "Protocol is there for a reason."

The older cop was back at the car, writing the report. He watched to see the new recruit holding his arms in the air.

"Hey bud, are you inquiring as to how we do our job?" said the other paramedic, who also had been writing a report. "You idiots were knocking on doors. Clearly you missed something on the way in here, but that call came in when we were on the other side of town. This kid is about as dead as a dead kid can be."

"Neither of you really checked, then. Did you know this is a reportable offense?" Chico had a vision of a news report he had once seen, an old woman rising up in the morgue.

The bigger paramedic was still squatting by the body. He crossed his arms over his legs. "You can check the pulse," he said.

Chico knelt down. "I guess I am showing you how to do your job," he said before his hand touched the child's neck.

The object that had once been a living child was taut like a balloon and soft, chilled even under the sun. It had not been apparent from where Chico was standing, but the spaces that the girl's eyes had once occupied were hollow and dark with rot. Chico's fingers pressed searchingly into the flesh of the neck, which offered no resistance. The skin was already weakening to the point where a slight push would send his hand through the front of the trachea and onto the girl's knobbed spine. The child was aspic.

The bigger paramedic said something and stood. His partner responded to him and looked at Chico, waiting. Across the parking lot, a figure emerged from a room, got into a car, and drove away. Chico removed his hand from the dead child's neck. "I'm sorry," he said. The man waved him off.

The older officer was there then, talking into his two-way. "Let's go," he said. "I'll drive." He leaned over and thumped Chico on the back with an open palm. The older officer clearly saw Chico as a novice, which he was, fresh from the academy and from high school before that.

They headed for the next call, a noise complaint that seemed to have been resolved prior to their arrival. On the way, Chico saw that both of his hands were slick with algae. He nearly wiped them on his pressed uniform pants, then stopped, instead resting his hands palms up on his knees. His hands dried, and he washed them hours later, nearly six hours later, when he was alone.

A few days passed before they paid a visit to David's family home.

15

NO DOMESTIC DISPUTE between Franny and David had inspired the removal of their wedding rings. She would take hers off at work when she was giving scalp massages. Once, she thought she had lost the ring, but she found it in the treatment room on a candleholder David had made for her during a personal failure of a pottery class he had taken the year he lost his job. After she found her ring, she started leaving it at home.

David didn't take any specific satisfaction from seeing a ring on his wife's finger. He thought about the day they first met, outside the grocery store during a similarly long winter. Her boot had slipped and she skidded down the sidewalk, kicking forward and losing her balance, pulling the long side of the rolling cart down onto her legs. David had been walking behind her and was startled at the movement. He stepped back in surprise, which gave her a clear path to the ground.

She went down hard, bouncing on the landing. He ran forward to pull the cart off her legs while she rubbed her thigh. "Jesus," she said. She watched David lower his own bags and pilot one of the cart's wheels into a groove in the pavement. He wore khaki pants that stretched across his rear end. Their grocery bags were mixed together in the confusion, and he loaded his items with hers into the cart. She saw a saint's medal glinting from a chain around his neck and felt poorly about taking the Lord's name in front of a religious man. "Thank you," she said.

"Your milk split," he said, lifting the dripping gallon.

She braced herself against the ground and stood. "Thank you for helping me," she said.

"You'll need another gallon." He watched her lift a foot and rotate her ankle in a slow circle, testing it. "I can get you one if you want to stay here."

"I've never had a man buy me milk."

"I'd like to be the first," he said. He realized that they were flirting, which was something he had seen and possibly experienced but had never understood in the moment as he did right then. Once, in college, he had told a woman that he enjoyed her scent, but he had seen it as an honest compliment, the kind one adult delivers to another, and not a statement given to promote a favorable reaction, a flirtatious statement, potentially garnering affection. "I would be honored to be the first," he said.

Whenever anyone heard the story of Franny and David's first meeting, they would ask why he hadn't caught her there in the grocery store parking lot. He would claim he hadn't been close enough. Years later he would stand next to a kiln and hope the objects inside would drastically change shape. They emerged as they had entered, amateur and uneven, too small, colored like wet sand.

David's wedding ring came off before Franny's, in their fifth year of marriage, a time of great stress in his life. He had lost his dental license the year before, and they had just moved in with his father. He found he had been fussing with the ring, turning it round and round on his finger until his skin flamed, the distressed red band suggesting allergy.

Then they both left their rings together at home and forgot where they ended up. Franny hoped they weren't in the basement. David forgot about them.

16.

DAVID SAT on the front stoop. The dead bolt was not electrified, he was sure. He was fairly sure. There was no evidence to suggest that the dead bolt was electrified, and it was more reasonable to assume that in fact it was not.

It was a bright day for winter, unusual too because of a drizzling rain that fell without cloud cover. David's eyes were spangled by sunlight. It seemed that the ground was moving, but then he looked closer and saw that the motion was created by black ants crawling from a crack in the walk, up the stairs, across the porch, and into a gap in the foundation, into the house. The ants were small enough and the drizzle light enough that a connection between the two would be rare indeed, though the ants moved sluggishly out of their hibernation. He wondered how an ant would celebrate the event of a raindrop, if it would survive the impact. David's body felt wrapped in a thin layer of cellophane.

He put his face close to the ground and found one ant. The creature walked unevenly, hefting a crumb larger than its body. It bumped into a pebble, the kind that might wedge in the tread of a boot, and began the slow journey around it. David pitied the ant and understood it. He took a tissue from his pocket and laid it down before the ant. After some coaxing, the ant stepped onto the tissue, pausing, pressing on. David slid his hand underneath and, moving low to the ground, stepped, crouching, up the stairs to the point where the line of ants vanished into the house. He shook the tissue close to the line, and the ant landed near. It touched the other ants with the tips of its mandibles, and they paused and touched the first ant before continuing on their way. David noticed that the crumb had fallen loose during transport. He examined the tissue and the porch at the point where he had released the ant. When he looked back at the line, he couldn't tell which ant he had moved. It was too late.

The dead bolt did not spark his hand on the way back inside, but he still did not feel safe. He considered the ways in which a wire could be secured to the bolt's knob, improving the safety of the door should the bolt at any point become electrified and a grounding element be unavailable.

He washed his hands upstairs, looking at the beauty products that still surrounded Franny's side of the sink. One bottle claimed to be a vacuum device for blackheads. He opened it and found a pump mechanism that dispensed an opalescent cream. Dabbing the cream on his forehead, he picked up another jar, a moisturizer with royal jelly. He wasn't sure how a jelly could be royal, but he removed its lid anyway and spread the cream under his chin. He picked up the tube of retinol eye cream she kept behind her toothbrush and smeared it over his eyes. He removed his clothes and sprinkled acetone-free nail polish remover on his pubic hair and worked it in at the roots.

His eyelids stung. He opened a precious-looking prismatic glass jar with a clear gel inside and smeared the gel on his testicles.

He sprayed her perfume on the back of his tongue. It made him retch, and he gripped the sink, coughing and spitting toward the drain. The perfume's fragrance was of flowers and some kind of light powder, but it tasted like cheap gin. It coated his tongue and cheeks and sank into his body. He splashed water into his mouth, but it served only to spread the flavor. He regarded his face in the mirror. Red welts were rising on his eyelids and neck. He resisted the urge to touch them.

Crouching down, he opened the cabinets under the sink. He pulled out bottles of cleanser, gallon jugs of shampoo and conditioner Franny had borrowed or taken from work, the box of Franny's pills. David counted ten months' worth of pills, ten stickers bearing Franny's name, twenty plastic hinges, hundreds of tabs of foil behind which hid hundreds of pills that meant nothing at all. A dental water jet attached to a turquoise-colored plastic box whirred when he plugged it in. David lay down and pressed his hands against the blind underside of the sink. He opened a jug of shampoo and emptied its contents over his body. The shampoo was a translucent blue and felt cold at first, but it warmed protectively and lathered a bit when he rubbed it. It covered his body and held him. He tried to crawl under the sink but could not fit his shoulders through the door. Instead, he lay with his head inside the paper-lined womb of the cabinet, its frame a wooden pillow under his head, the dental water jet whirring like a lullaby.

17

DAVID STOOD beside his wife at their wedding reception. The event was well attended, in part because it was held at an Old Country Buffet during the dinner rush. Their invited guests didn't seem to mind the $7.99 charge. David had just taken on more debt by buying his dental office, in addition to what he paid monthly for his mother's care, in addition to her old legal bills. Franny and David had been married by the justice that afternoon, and she was still wearing the white lace skirt that made her knees look like the speckled hams under heat lamps at the buffet. Patrons of the restaurant wandered into their corner to shake David's hand and tell Franny that she looked lovely. A child gave Franny a fistful of gummy bears from the ice cream station.

The young husband of one of David's dental hygienists brought a cooler of beer. David's father returned from the dinner line with a plate heaped with meat. "Pig to pork," he said. He shook his son's hand and picked up a rolled silverware napkin from the table. "Live with meaning and die old."

Three empty plates at a table held corsages as symbols of

Franny's parents and David's mother, who had moved herself into a women's home when David was very young. He couldn't recall exactly when his mother had gone to the home, and he and his father rarely visited. When they did, she always gave David something she had made, a card or ornament, out of the same type of construction paper her son had used in his kindergarten class. Once, the keepsake was a picture she had drawn of David in red and blue marker.

His mother had been a math teacher and was the only truly calculating element across the entire course of David's life. She expressed no interest in ever meeting Franny. On their wedding day, his mother called the Old Country Buffet and the newlyweds passed the phone back and forth while standing at the hostess station.

Everyone got a little too drunk and kept eating. They put away plates of meat and baked beans and iceberg salads with ranch dressing. A distant cousin ate only creamed corn. David and Franny sat at the table with his father and the hygienist and her husband. David's father lifted a spoon of mashed potatoes. "Once, this was all underground," he said. The hygienist's husband ringed his big arm around David's neck and told him it was good to marry a strong woman who could get herself out of trouble. David imagined Franny pinned under a grain thresher, hefting it overhead into a hayloft.

At the end of the evening, Franny placed a dish of pudding by one of her parents' memorial plates and started to cry. The guests had mostly left, save for a patron of the restaurant named Chuck who produced a flask of whiskey and sat with his back to the wall. Franny wiped her eyes with her mother's memorial napkin and took a pull from the offered flask.

That night, Franny and David lay in bed together, immobile from the pleasures of the buffet. She slept, and he examined the muscles twitching under her skin. In those early years, Franny's body lacked the twin mysteries of scent and softness that had initially allured and eventually drove him from the bedrooms of his few previous girlfriends. His wife's scent that night was of a wet rock, as if she had been created from the stream that ran behind his childhood home.

18.

OVER A LIFETIME of experience, David's mother learned that institutional food was more or less the same, regardless of the location, purpose, or quality of the institution in question. If they could make a fruit out of a chunk of Styrofoam, they would do it. David's mother felt certain that she had once eaten a synthetic pear served to her by the institution. She could discern the pear's flavor but it registered only vaguely, as if she was experiencing the pear under sedation or in a dream. Its texture was of a wet sponge soaked in chemicals.

She fumbled to peel the crimped foil on her orange juice container. It evaded her fingers, which felt thicker with every year's birthday card she opened from her son, her old fingers failing even to separate paper from adhesive. He sent old cards, even a few she had given him for his own birthdays. The other ladies read them to her. David sometimes sent the letters her sister had written before she passed. This was before she settled into a less-demarcated timeline of growth and weakening. Her hands lost their power to the point where she had trouble turning a doorknob.

David's mother fantasized about being able to turn door-knobs. There was the unyielding chill of metal under her strong hand, which gripped and turned so easily, feeling through her fingers the internal mechanism of the door. Her blindness heightened her sense of touch, allowing her to experience an even purer form of pleasure. Each joint in her body moved with a similar efficiency and silence. Shoulder and elbow, wrist, knuckles, fingertips; synchronous. She slowed down the motion in her memory of it, fingers grasping, tucking under the metal with such precision. She could feel the seam where metal met turning metal, the knob's joints meeting her own. In her fantasy of it, she felt so strong that she could rip the knob off the door and hold it in her hand like a stone.

The women at this particular institution guided David's mother through open doors in the distant way that they would guide an old woman at any institution. They sat her at empty tables and helped with her playing cards. The ridges and grooves in the cards greeted the sense of touch in her hands, which she still refused to admit was dimming.

19

ONE NEW MESSAGE. Three saved messages. First new message. From, phone number three three zero, three two three, seven four nine eight. Received, November eleventh at two-thirty-two p.m.

Hello, David, this is Reginald Chico. I'm going to need to come by and ask you a few questions about the case. It's important that we clear up some things to close the file. It's an open file now. Well, we opened the file. Please give me a call if you won't be home. I figure you'll be home.

Message erased. First saved message. From, phone number three three zero, four five four, eight seven zero one. Received, September fourth at nine-forty-three a.m.

Hello, this call is for Frances. This is Andrew at the Precious Memories preservation department. I am calling to report that your order is complete and ready for pickup. Thank you for your patience and have a wonderful day.

Replay, four. Erase, seven. Return call, eight. Save, nine. More options, zero. Message erased. Next message. From, phone

number three three zero, eight four five, three four three three.
Received, October fifteenth at eleven-eleven a.m.

Hey. Please wash and prep the vegetables before I get home.
We're in a hurry. Sorry. See you.

Saved. There are no more messages. Main menu. Listen,
one. Send, two. Personal options, three. Call, eight. Exit, star.

First saved message. From, phone number three three
zero, eight four five, three four three three. Received, October
fifteenth at eleven-eleven a.m.

Hey. Please wash and prep the vegetables before I get home.
We're in a hurry. Sorry. See you.

Saved. There are no more messages. Main menu. Listen,
one. Send, two. Personal options, three. Call, eight. Exit, star.

First saved message. From, phone number three three
zero, eight four five, three four three three. Received, October
fifteenth at eleven-eleven a.m.

Hey. Please wash and prep the vegetables before I get home.
We're in a hurry. Sorry. See you.

Saved. There are no more messages. Main menu. Listen,
one. Send, two. Personal options, three. Call, eight. Exit, star.
To indicate your choice, press the number of the option you
wish to select. Whenever you need more information about
the options, press zero for help. You can interrupt these instructions at any time by pressing a key to make your selection.

20

CHICO knocked on the front door for some time before moving to the window. David lifted the sash and held out his hand for Chico to take as he crawled in. The detective was a thin man, but it took some leverage to pull him through. He moved as if struggling against considerable weight, and the two men had to take a break in the middle of the action, while the detective's legs still rested on the ground outside.

The detective tried to find a toehold on the brick wall. He grunted and sighed. "You've got to get that door fixed," he said.

"It may be electrified."

"I know. I know you think it may be electrified." He wedged his foot into a crack in the foundation and hefted himself in.

They sat on the floor together. Chico leaned against the wall and coughed. "The doctor claims I have a good heart," he said. He removed his muddy shoes and placed them carefully on the wood floor beside the rug.

David produced one of the police blankets and made a nest around Chico's feet.

"Thank you," said the detective. "Cold outside. I believe I

walked through half a pond in your driveway. Have you examined the drainage out there?"

"Can I offer you something to drink?"

"No thanks, David. But thank you. Thank you. I came to ask you a few questions. The department prefers that I travel with a partner, but I felt you were uncomfortable with Officer Riley. I came alone today to ask you some questions." He tucked the blanket around his feet. "Would that be amenable to you?"

David nodded.

"Very good." Chico leaned to the side and extracted a writing pad and utensil from his back pocket. "You're wearing your bathrobe, David."

"That's right."

"And your slippers are wet. You've been outside?"

"Sure," David said. "Yes."

"Where did you go?"

"I walked on the grass after the ice storm."

Chico nodded, making a note.

"I like the sound of the ice. I was wearing pants at the time."

"Pants," Chico transcribed. "Jeans, or pants?"

"Pants." David half stood, but didn't complete the action and ended up bending at the waist over the detective.

"Did you have somewhere you needed to be?" Chico asked, leaning back to meet David's eyes.

"I thought we had been talking for a while."

"We just started talking."

David looked at the hall clock, which had stopped. "It is possible we have only just begun to talk. I'm sorry." He sat down again.

"The apology is unnecessary." Chico maintained his extended level of eye contact.

David regarded him as a careful man who took regular trips to the doctor. It seemed easier to trust a careful man.

Chico turned back to his notepad. "Did you love your wife?"

"I love my wife."

"Did you two ever have any big arguments? Fights? Shouting, throwing objects at each other? Physical contact?"

"Not really, no."

"It's a common phenomenon."

"She threw a newspaper at me once, but she apologized."

Chico turned the page and kept writing. "Did Franny enjoy her job?"

"It was half a newspaper, really. Less than half. Just the sports section."

"Did she have many friends?"

"Of the Saturday paper, you know. We're talking eight sheets of paper here."

"That sounds very minor, David."

"I wouldn't have noticed if she hadn't knocked my glasses off. She messed up the center bar. I had to tape them up. They were never like they were before."

"You wear glasses."

"I've always worn glasses." David touched his own face. "I'm wearing them now."

Chico closed his notepad. "David," he said. "What happened to your wife?"

"When?" asked David. "When?" He lay down on the floor, at Chico's feet. He saw a paper bag on a shelf. The ceiling was a strange thing to see, and David realized that he had never lain flat on the floor in his own home. The ceiling's surface was dusty and smooth, forming an angled plane with the wall. It looked like it was a cold surface, one he could press his face against. He thought about how no dust should rightly form on the ceiling and how strange it was that dust did somehow populate up there, the webbed pockets of dust texturing in the corners. David imagined that if one or two specks of dust impossibly clung to the minute crevices of the ceiling, then another piece of dust and another could attach to those first colonizers, and in the course of fifty years, that string of codependent detritus could make its own meaningful line, stretching toward but never reaching the floor, existing beyond the reach of brooms and rags. He remembered how his mother would dust the corners of that very room with a damp rag. She wore another damp rag tied over her mouth for the sake of her allergies. He thought of the individual path of one such piece of dust: into the rag and washed down the sink, affixed to the interior of a pipe for a few weeks or months, time becoming less relevant to the speck than time was before—which is to say not at all relevant or perhaps negatively relevant—the speck washed free after some time, proceeding through the mess of pipes and into an underground tank, sinking through sludge to become sludge yet remaining an individual speck, having no original qualities yet remaining unique, sinking or aloft, present in the world.

21.

DAVID AWOKE ON THE FLOOR. It was dark outside, and his shoulder was too stiff to move. He felt bruised. He didn't remember falling asleep. Over the hours that had passed, his bones had settled and pinned him down. When he moved his legs, he felt the blood coursing to his lower body. His sore shoulder flushed and tingled as he sat up.

It had been a long time since he had needed his heavy winter coat, and he hadn't looked for it in years. He tended to wear his robe for trips to the mailbox or a light jacket for walks around the neighborhood. He hadn't taken note of the temperature or what he was wearing on his recent trip to the post office.

The coat was not in the downstairs closet. He checked the closets upstairs, the bedroom closets, the linen closet, the closet in the bathroom. He found the extra towels and considered wrapping them around his hands and arms and face. He forgot what he was looking for and checked the medicine cabinet in the bathroom. He remembered and dug through his side of the bedroom dresser. He found long underwear, jeans, a sweatshirt, and a ballpoint pen. At the back of one drawer was a scarf his mother had mailed from the home for women. David removed his robe and pajamas and put on the clothes.

Under the bed, he found winter clothes that had been vacuum sealed in large plastic pouches. When he opened one, it expanded and released the odor of a wet stone. David put his face into the pouch and held it there. His face touched one of Franny's favorite coats from the previous winter, one she had worn nearly every day. The coat was sewn from a bronze-colored fabric and gathered at intervals, giving the wearer the look of having stacked multiple cast-metal hoops up the body.

Her black winter gloves were stuffed in the coat's pockets. His hand was like a child's in the glove. He imagined Franny putting the gloves there in her pockets to surprise herself for the next season. He kept the gloves on and counted five more sealed pouches under the bed, each holding pillows or duvet covers or more of Franny's coats and sweaters. He lowered his face to the bronze coat again and inhaled its scent before spreading it out over the bed. One of his old jackets was at the bottom of the pouch, a blue and ivory ski jacket with a red zipper, something he had worn in college. He put it on.

His shoes felt strange on his feet, and he saw that he had forgotten his socks. The sock drawer was empty save for the velvet box containing a rare coin given to him by his uncle when he was ten years old. David hadn't opened the drawer in at least a year. He couldn't think of a more intuitive place to store socks beyond the sock drawer, but Franny made judgment calls that he tended not to understand immediately. Dust lined the drawer. David opened the velvet box and touched the surface of the coin with the tips of his gloved fingers. There was a pattern of stars ringing the relief sculpture, circling a woman with either a clutch of arrows or an antique tooth extractor held to her chest. He put the coin back in its velvet box and put the velvet box back in the drawer.

Franny's sock drawer was empty as well. She usually kept soft cloth bags of lavender with her socks and undergarments, but they were gone. Her drawer looked as if it had been scrubbed. David wondered if the police had taken the socks, if the firefighters had, the workers, the girls from the salon. He opened other drawers to find the clothes folded neatly.

He found one pair of Franny's socks wrapped around a pipe in the linen closet. They were distended as a result of their insulation duty. They were kneesocks, cold as the water that flowed through the pipe they had insulated for years, pulled tightly around the exposed pipe and knotted twice each. The knots were difficult to loosen and the act chilled his hands. They smelled like rusting metal. The socks featured orange rust at the points where the fabric stretched the farthest. David sat on the floor and put the socks on, then the shoes. He wiped the gloves on his jeans and stood.

22

DAVID AND FRANNY went camping together only once, at a campground that allowed cars and firewood and coolers. The cars bellied up to the individual camping spots, protecting the rock-lined fire pits like steely animal flanks. They heard a generator powering a television. Franny observed the activity and light and said that she had always thought of camping as strapping one's provisions to one's back and walking into the woods. David had never camped before, but he imagined others walking, feet falling uncertainly on new territory, eyes scanning the ground ahead, stopping occasionally to drink water from a jug and lean back to look at the canopied trees above. At the car campground, Franny and David walked to the edge of a lake. The water shifted to cover and uncover rocks and shells on the beach. They decided that if the lake was a magic trick, the trick was that there were shells despite the fact that they were standing a long day's worth of driving from any ocean, ten hours of driving, weeks of walking. He put his arm around her, and she sang a quiet song about a man who takes a journey.

Day trips were more their style. There was a high concentration of antique shops in the area, and the two spent most of their time exploring, flanked by retirees. Franny would leave David at the boxes of tin saints' medals and return to show him photos and postcards she had found in the shop's recesses.

Despite never experiencing organized religion beyond his mother's plastic rosaries, he had an abiding reverence for Saint Apollonia, who, around the year 249, suffered the indignity of having every single one of her teeth bashed in by persecutors of Christians. Apollonia was supposed to be burned toothless at the stake but instead launched herself into the fire, an act pardoned by Saint Augustine, who noted the suicidal action of Apollonia's leap and forgave her and similar martyred individuals, for they acted on God's command. "Not through human caprice but on the command of God, not erroneously but through obedience," Augustine wrote. The classical image of Apollonia was of a beautiful girl holding antique extractors in which a tooth was delicately grasped. She was the patron saint of dentistry, and David collected her prayer cards and medals the way he had collected coins as a kid. Adding to a collection always seemed to have a larger point, which could be appreciated even when he was the only one handing over the cash for the rounds of silver and tin stamped with the saint's calm face, extractors aloft as her symbol of martyrdom.

When he found an Apollonia charm, he would bring it home in a folded brown bag and leave it on the kitchen table. Franny liked to examine them on her own. She would thread a piece of ribbon through the hoop at the top as if it was a necklace for display, holding it up to the light. Then she would place it back inside its paper bag for David to find later. He stored them on a high bookshelf in the living room.

Franny grew up with religion and occasionally observed its traditions. One cold evening, the two of them walked to a church down the hill and received the sign of the cross on their foreheads with ashes. She scrubbed hers off the next morning before work, but David could feel his own mark as if it was still a flame. He left it on for days, until it smudged and buried itself in the individual pores on his forehead, sinking grease in the furrows between his eyes, giving him the brindled pallor of a man carved from stone.

23.

DAVID PREFERRED to brew a pot of coffee and leave it to fill the house with its scent, but such a move required that he find the coffeemaker and the filters and then the coffee itself. The police officer had left the instant grounds out, and David put them away. The coffeemaker was under the counter by the sink, and the filters were behind a line of cans in the pantry. He found the coffee in the freezer, rolled into a fist-size brick and secured with rubber bands. He had trouble gripping the coffee spoon with gloves on, so he removed one glove and pressed his bare hand on the countertop. His bruised body and brain were confused by the darkness outside and the smell of coffee. It had felt as if it was still evening until he started making the coffee, when it began to feel like morning. He didn't have a clock to check.

Regardless, it made no sense to leave the house, whatever hour it was. He tried to rationalize his way back into bed with the fact that he could rest underneath Franny's coat, which smelled strongly of a wet rock, though the scent surely had already mixed and diluted on the bed with David's own scents from the previous days. It seemed important to take a shower, or sleep and wait for the sun. The coffee brewed and dripped, and he thought about drinking it in the shower or pouring it into a pouch so he could have it while lying in bed. The temptations occurred as he blew the steam from his first cup.

In the days when he would get up early and go to work, he took his coffee to enjoy in the shower, a wet warm surrounded by warm wet. Sometimes he sat down on the tiled floor, his back against the shower's glass door. Drops of water would splash the surface of the coffee. It had been a secret pleasure.

David missed the smell of sanitized dental tools mingling with coffee. He would have his hygienist come in an hour before him each day and prepare the place, laying the clean tools out on metal trays at each station, covering each tray with a sanitized plastic bib. The smell was of new metal and smooth plastic, the opposite of the ground teeth and dry socket rot that would drift through the office throughout the day.

He had enjoyed his peaceful half hour before patients arrived. The front desk assistant would put on the easy-listening station and David walked through his office, sipping coffee from a thermos and observing each room, enjoying its spotless smell. Sometimes he sat in the examination chair and visualized himself as one of his own patients. He reclined the chair fully and saw the patterns within the ceiling tile. He listened in on the receptionist talking to one of the hygienists about college football.

It was hard to admit that those days were over, but it was hard to admit that any days were over, that the days themselves didn't stretch like pulled taffy and sag to the floor.

He wiped a layer of dust from the old coffeemaker. The machine had been a wedding gift and was the type with a removable top portion for easy cleaning. When David was dumping the filter in the trash, he saw a piece of paper taped on the back of the reservoir. The paper was half the size of an index card and featured typewritten words:

```
YOUR FATE IS SEALED WITH GLUE I HAVE BOILED
IN A VAT. I SLOPPED IT ON AN ENVELOPE AND
MAILED IT TO YOUR MOTHER'S WOMB.
```

David pulled the taped card off the coffeemaker and turned it over. The card bore no other marks, besides a lightened patch on the upper edge where the Scotch tape made contact with the paper. The card seemed old enough to have been sold with the appliance, but its condition could also have been attributed to resting on the hot surface. The edges of the card were crisp, without even a rounded darkening suggesting that they had been used to excavate underneath a fingernail.

David thought about calling the police, but then he imagined handing them the piece of paper, explaining that he had found it while making coffee. He decided that such a discovery would be best dealt with privately. Likely the threat had been stuck on by whoever gave them the gift, as a joke or not as a joke, but still beyond David's concern years after the fact. He could not begin to think about the number of things that were truly beyond his concern, the hundreds of thousands of things.

The house was a void. Its dark hallway beckoned. Curtains in the living room stood like sentry ghosts. Each room featured an obvious kind of silence that suggested invisible occupants holding their collective breath. He folded the tape over on the card and pressed the adhesive to the paper surface. He placed the card face-down on the counter, put his glove back on, and opened the door.

24.

SNOW MELTED through the seams in David's thin shoes and soaked ice water into Franny's socks and between his toes. When he walked down the driveway, he saw that Franny's car was gone from its usual spot in front of the garage. Someone had taken it and left behind an expanse of gravel and murk in the middle of the snow. He walked down the hill and toward the main road. A runner nodded as he passed, wearing what looked like a full wet suit under shorts.

Walking, David thought of himself as a dotted arc on a map of the world, dropping a plumb line toward some sandy beach. He imagined moving south as a tired crow might fly, over woods, stopping to rest on power lines overlooking gas stations. If David were a crow, he would stay away from trees, preferring man-made structures. He would be a friendly kind of crow, brave enough to communicate with other crows. They could hop around a dish of warm water. The snow would melt to a filthy slush around the Mason-Dixon Line and give way to the clean, sun-drenched variety of winter he imagined was general in Florida. He would be a crow on the sand. His warmer downy feathers would molt and float away as he flew.

The streets were empty, save for a few late-night or early-morning runners and the rare sweep of headlights. He saw dead leaves on the trees for what felt like the first time, though of course he had seen dead leaves in the past. He tried to think. The leaves were speckled with wilt. They hung from the trees like leather pelts.

The laundromat was the only occupied place. Its lights cast a men's-room shade of yellow over the street. David went into the warm room and took a seat by the door. He remembered that very laundromat from his childhood. Once a year, his mother would take down all the curtains and bundle them up and spend the afternoon watching them spin in the industrial-size washing machines. His sister was there for a few trips, quiet in her stroller, reaching for David's outstretched finger with the arm that wasn't tucked inside her corduroy coveralls. The laundromat was the same as it had always been. The brand of detergent stocked in the automatic dispenser had changed, but the dispenser itself remained original to the space. The old pinball machine remained, wherein the silver balls had been tasked with escaping a haunted house.

Eight carts had been lined up against a wall of dryers, their wheels locked. The carts were filled with laundry. Another person was working on them, a woman, older than David by a wide margin and wearing enough layers of earth-toned clothing that the edges of her body were unclear. All of the carts seemed to belong to her. There was a small child curled up in one of them, sleeping. The woman took a sweater out of one basket and pulled it on over the two sweaters she already wore. She didn't look at David, and their silence became an energy. He removed his shoes and socks and padded barefoot to a dryer. He put them in the machine. "Warming up," he said.

Her face was like a loaf of bread. "Back already," she said.

"What's that?"

She walked across the line of spinning dryers, peering into each. Opening one, she dug in, pulled out a pair of socks, and tossed them to David. MARLON was stitched into the fabric of the sock's cuff. "Welcome home," she said.

He put the socks on. They were warm. "What's your name?"

She extracted a T-shirt from under the child's bare feet in the cart and tossed it into a washing machine. "Shelly."

"Who's Marlon?"

Clearing her throat, she folded a sweater and moved it to another basket. She rolled a basket to the side, slipped around it, and leaned toward him, plucking a piece of lint from his blue and ivory ski jacket. "Marlon's not around," she said, tucking the lint in her breast pocket and returning to her folding task. The shirts she worked on seemed generally mismatched to one another, like she had cleared a clearance rack at the Catholic ladies' thrift store down the street. As she folded a long-sleeved shirt, David saw that it was slashed down the breast in a vertical line starting from under the collar and terminating five inches lower.

"It's cold out," he said, digging in his pockets for quarters. The skin on the back of his hand rubbed raw on the frozen fabric of his jeans.

Shelly stood close enough that he could tell she was chewing fruit-flavored gum. Pushing the empty quarter tray halfway, she smacked the dryer's front panel with a practiced palm. The machine began to mumble with activity. She regarded David sidelong and thumped the center of his chest with the heel of her hand.

He coughed. "Nice trick."

"It's exclusively a night trick." She took a pair of pants out of another dryer and pulled them on under her long brown skirt. When she tugged down the skirt's waist to button the pants, he saw that she was wearing at least two more pairs. The waists of the pants layered in circles like rings in a tree. She readjusted her skirt and focused again on her baskets, consolidating clothes by color, picking out a sweater that featured a wide dark stain around the collar and tossing it into a machine that was already full of water.

"It's too cold to be out," she said. "Stay where it's warm and safe."

The water tinted pink around the sweater soaking alone in the wash. "You'll have a hard time wearing that one," David said.

"Think of a time you've felt warm and *un*safe," she said. "Try to think of such a time." As she spoke, she took a batch of clean clothes from a clicking dryer, draped a warm blanket over the child in the cart, and loaded the rest into an empty cart. She rolled the cart to the high folding table, and she ducked underneath to find a plastic step stool. She held the table and stepped onto the stool, then crouched to the rolling cart and began transferring handfuls of jeans and shirts and sweaters and blouses to the table. Organizing the clothes in a loose pile, she took a pair of slacks from the top. She stretched the slacks between two hands and smoothed them with her palm, then leaned in close and examined the fabric. There was a scorch mark on the fly, which she ignored, focusing on a stray thread that emerged from a pocket.

David watched her fold the clothes. He looked out the window and at the clock on the wall. After a while he opened the dryer that contained his shoes and socks. The canvas on his shoes was hot and wet and smelled like pancakes, but Franny's rust-ringed socks were dry. He removed Marlon's socks and tucked them atop the machine.

Shelly was folding a slashed-up shirt as carefully as the rest, buttoning it to the neck and holding the collar taut.

"Thanks for the free dry," David said, taking a seat to put his shoes on. "Are you here most nights?"

She lifted her eyes from her work and saw him lacing up his shoes, hunched over himself in the plastic chair, his head tipped toward her, face reddening against the strain as if he was holding his breath or trying not to expel gas, and she laughed at the sight of him. She held the counter to steady herself and laughed. The noise startled him. He stood and tried to back up at the same time, tripping sideways over the chair. It made her laugh harder, the sight of him holding the chair and tripping across his untied shoes and finally staggering half laced out of the laundromat. It would be foolish to be afraid of the woman's laughter, but David could easily put reason to feeling surprised and unsettled. He admitted to these emotions in the dark and limped home.

25.

IT WAS STILL FULLY NIGHT when David re-
turned to his street. His wet shoes had frozen again, their trailing laces gathering a snowy coating like a naked wick in wax.
The warmth in Franny's old socks had slipped away and the
bones in his feet were a stiff, burning cold. He kicked the shoes
off the moment he reached his porch steps. He had fashioned
a grounding wire for the doorknob earlier that day, and now he
safely tapped the frame with his socked foot. He detected an
energy, but when he reached for the knob, he felt no shock and
opened the door. Behind him, a pair of joggers crested the final hill and held hands as they navigated the icy road together.

He still had the laundromat's scent on his skin, an odor
that was supposedly the chemical essence of mountain air. His
empty home smelled like coffee and furniture polish and
paper. In the entry, the grandfather clock gave a few easy ticks
and stopped again. The flaps of a cardboard box at the base
of the stairs rustled in the opening door's breeze, and David
remembered the urine-soaked clothes inside. He emptied the

mess out on the porch and tossed the soiled box down the basement's dark stairs.

Upstairs, he removed his clothes and stood naked under the bathroom's warm light. He scooped the last of Franny's eye cream from its jar, which was so small that only the tip of his smallest finger fit inside. He spread the thimbleful of cream on his chest, where it warmed pleasantly. Inside a hinged pot he found a sparkling paste she might have used on her eyes or lips. It was an ivory color, and when he spread it on his mouth it tasted like mineral oil and pencil shavings. Wrapped around the base of the hinged pot was a thin piece of paper that reeled out like an old ticker tape when he loosened its sticky tab. It read:

```
I WILL CROSS-STITCH AN IMAGE OF YOUR FUTURE
HOME BURNING. I WILL HANG THIS IMAGE OVER YOUR
BED WHILE YOU SLEEP.
```

Released from its anchor, the paper sprang free and curled into the sink. One end was still attached to the fragile hinged jar, and he picked it off with his fingernail, flattening the thin page on the counter and considering it. His mother would buy cross-stitch patterns but never begin work on them, even at the women's home, where she had a seemingly endless span of time for artistic and other projects.

David considered the possibility that the threat had been included with the product from the manufacturer as a way to distract women from the amount of money they were spending on mineral oil and pencil shavings. Wiping the stinging product from his lips with the back of his hand, he wrapped the threat around the sink's faucet.

He got into bed but felt a low-level awareness of the threat curled up in the bathroom. He pulled a stack of magazines from the bedside table into bed with him, making a line between his body and the bathroom. The magazines and Franny's copper-colored coat insulated him, and he tucked his legs toward his chest. He imagined the words and images in the magazines rising up like a wall.

When he switched off the bedroom light, his eyes adjusted to the green glow of his electric shaver in the bathroom and he remembered how Franny's body shone when she came out of the bathroom to join him in bed at night, her skin a reflected emerald shade that inspired in him a vision of her rising from some stagnant pond and approaching him, robe flowing, eyes empty. Replaying the vision in a loop, he fell asleep and had no dreams.

26

DETECTIVE CHICO rang the front bell and waited. "There's a grounding wire on your door," he said pleasantly when David opened up. Chico tapped the wire with his boot. "Was this your doing?"

A woman stood next to Chico. She was bundled up. "This is Dr. Walls," said Chico. "She is a mental health professional."

The woman held out her gloved hand.

"Hello," David said, shaking it.

"Don't worry, sir," said Dr. Walls, squinting at him, removing her winter gloves though she was still outside. She extended her bare hand, and David shook it again. "I'm not here to commit you."

"We came by to have another talk about how you're doing," said Chico.

David wondered at the condition of Chico's teeth.

"Dr. Walls would like to know you. There's no harm in inviting us in."

"It's cold out here," Dr. Walls said, holding one bare hand

with the other. She had the kind of pale skin that turned trans-lucent in the winter.

David tracked the progression of her sluggish blood. He opened the door wider. "I could offer you some tea," he said.

"You could offer and we could accept," said Dr. Walls.

David led the way to the kitchen. The card with the first threat was still facedown on the kitchen counter, and he opened the silverware drawer and slid it underneath the butter knives. He removed a spoon and closed the drawer.

"Sugar?" he asked.

"Yes please," said Dr. Walls, who had picked up a news-paper from the kitchen table and was holding it close to her face. She unstuck a ballpoint pen that had been taped to the window frame over the table.

"You've got your sugar spoon all ready to go," Chico said.

David felt he could trust Chico about as much as he could trust any police detective who had made multiple trips to his home. David put the spoon in his robe pocket, set the pot of water on the range, and took the box of tea out from the pantry along with the bag of sugar.

"How have you been feeling?" Chico asked.

Placing the sugar on the counter, David slipped some tea bags into his robe pocket, opened the cabinet, and took down three cups and three saucers. He arranged each cup on a sau-cer and picked up the bag of sugar. "I'm fine. I went on a walk," he said, unrolling the bag. Inside, a scrap of paper peeked above the sugar line like a prize in a cereal box. David held the bag close to his chest and dropped his free hand into his pocket.

AMELIA GRAY

"Very good," said Chico. "I was worried you would be cooped up all season."

"Laying eggs," Dr. Walls said, rubbing her eyes.

David clutched the sugar spoon in his pocket. "My wife's car is gone."

"Yes," Chico said. "The bank confiscated the vehicle due to nonpayment." He tapped his shirt pocket and reached inside. "I can give you the number of the appropriate department to contact with your grievances."

"It doesn't matter," David said. "I mean, if that settled the debt, it doesn't matter. I didn't like that car."

Dr. Walls made a mark on the newspaper. "The light in here," she said.

The water on the stove pimpled with the pending boil. The spoon was cutting a ridge into David's palm and he loosened his grip and brought it out of his pocket. "Thank you for letting me know about the car," he said. He used the spoon to dig into the sugar mound, uncovering more of the paper. There was a word on it, a sentence. He turned his body, placing himself between Chico and the bag.

"We've been talking to a few coworkers of your wife," Chico said. "Nobody said anything against you, but they all did have the same issue."

"An issue." David dug around the piece of paper, trying to make unnoticeable motions, careful not to rip the page.

"They all mentioned the fact that you're never around. A few of them joked that they didn't think you really existed. Only one of them claimed to have even met you."

"They came over and cut my hair three weeks ago."

Chico looked at Dr. Walls, who set aside the newspaper

and produced a pad of sticky notes. She wrote something on one. The water came to a full boil while David was reaching his hand into the sugar bag to grasp the corner of the paper. He kept his back square between the bag and the detective.

"Who cut your hair?" Chico asked.

The page in the sugar was not a card or a strip, but a full piece of notebook paper. When he had unearthed enough of it, David closed the top edge of the page in his fist and pulled it out whole. The action spilled sugar on the counter, his robe, the floor, the range. The sugar blackened and burned under the pot of boiling water. In one motion, he stuffed the piece of paper into his pocket and leaned down to blow on the smoke rising from the burning sugar. "It was a whole group of them," he said. He felt the grains of sugar coating his hand and wiped it on his chest. "They seemed like nice girls. Maybe they were students. They were all young."

"The girls cut your hair."

David poured water into the cups and spooned sugar into one. Steam blushed the spoon's edge. "One cut my toenails. I told them all not to bother, but they said they were here to do it as a favor to my wife." The threat felt warm in his pocket.

"Could I get their names?" Chico asked.

"I don't know their names," David said. He reasoned that if he had left the threat in the sugar, it might have dissolved and vanished. It was too important to be ruled by the normal properties of paper. Taking hold of it had been important.

Dr. Walls was beside him. "David, your hair is past your ears."

"It was longer," David said, handing her a cup. He touched the fuzzed nape of his neck. "You wouldn't believe."

"Where do you keep the tea?" she asked.

David patted the front of his robe, produced one of the bags, and dropped it into her cup. He had the sense that this woman was here to trick him. He didn't trust the things she said or the way she watched him. He crossed his arms, covering his pockets so that she couldn't reach in. The woman went back to sit at the table in the seat where guests sat, the one without a place mat. She was trying to be polite. David slipped the other tea bags into the other cups.

"I'm sorry we're asking so many questions," Chico said, accepting his tea. "I'm sure you want to get to the bottom of this as much as we do."

"Important items have special properties," David said.

"You have been so helpful," said Dr. Walls.

"I believe I've maintained a tradition of cooperation with members of local law enforcement and public works operatives," he said. "I believe that civilians ought not fear the guiding hand of the state." He lifted the cup to his lips.

"What was that page you pulled out of the bag of sugar?" Chico asked.

David effused a small amount of bile into his tea.

"Good God," said Dr. Walls.

"What is your name?" David asked the woman. He wiped his face with his sleeve. "What is your full name?"

The woman's teacup rattled on its saucer, though she was touching neither cup nor saucer. He saw her leg jiggling the table from underneath. "Marie Walls," the woman said.

"Marie," he said. "I'm sorry about all this."

"It's all right, David."

"I haven't been the same since my wife left."

"David," she said.

"I hate to state the obvious," said Chico, "but you vomited into that cup after I asked you a question."

"David," Marie said. Her face elongated before him. Her eyebrows went first, pinching a delicate fold into her forehead. Her eyelids snapped up to follow and she tipped her head back slightly to accommodate the movement. She observed him from behind her cheekbones.

David was holding the paper protectively in his pocket. "It was nothing," he said. "It was a piece of the bag that fell into the sugar. I felt ashamed to serve the sugar to guests with a piece of the bag loose inside." He attempted a religious convert kind of gaze with the detective, but Chico's eye contact was stronger. It was clear that in a past life the detective had been a phone booth beside an empty highway. David felt the page wilting in his warm hand. The sugar stuck to his palm.

From the corner of his eye he could see that Marie was nodding. "Such a good host," she said.

"A good host," Chico said. He was making the kind of eye contact employed by officers of the law. He had once been a mechanical crane that hauled beams to the top of a skyscraper.

David tipped his ruined tea out in the sink, took the paper out of his pocket, and laid it on the table. Chico stood beside him and read it aloud:

I WILL STRIP THE BARK FROM A TREE AND MAKE YOU NEW CLOTHES. YOU WILL WEAR THESE CLOTHES AS YOU WANDER THE FOREST FOR FOURTEEN YEARS. YOUR FATHER WILL DIE WATCHING THE SKY AND YOUR MOTHER WILL FORGET YOUR NAME.

Chico stopped reading, but David could tell he was looking over it again, memorizing it. The man had no visible reaction beyond his jaw moving slightly down and to the left behind his closed mouth. It was enough for David to know that he should not have trusted either of his visitors.

"I don't know what to make of it," David said.

"There are more like this?"

"No," David said. "I found it there before. I was afraid to move it."

"I should take it with me," Chico said, pulling on his gloves and holding one out for the threat.

"What's happening?" Marie asked, bracing herself to stand.

"Official police business," Chico said.

David held the threat close to his chest. "There's no police business. I can't let you have this."

Chico made no initial response, but his jaw moved again within his closed mouth. He was tonguing the surface of his molars. He seemed exceptionally calm. "This could be considered evidence," he said.

"There's no reason why it would be. My wife was probably playing a prank on me, and she forgot about it." David worried that he was talking too fast. Correcting the error would be simple enough but would require talking more to the man, who was probing the grooves in his teeth as if they contained an illuminating secret. "I usually don't take sugar in my tea," David said, slower, moderated, trying his best to sound reasonable by employing a reasonable voice, "so there was no reason for me to look here. I don't usually take sugar."

"This could be an important piece of evidence," said Chico.

Marie had abandoned her teacup and stood by Chico's side. "Goodness," she said, replacing her thin glasses with thicker ones and reading the page. "Classic transferred umbilical addiction. ICD-10 F20. The coupled individual fears the opposing parental unit and conspires to destroy him or her."

"There's no reason why you wouldn't allow us to take this," Chico said.

"Or it's a ruse," Marie said.

"You've been nothing but helpful so far," Chico added. "Your attitude has helped to ease my mind regarding your status in this case."

David folded the paper in thirds. "Ease your mind."

"You're a person of interest, after all. That's normal procedure. You're only helping yourself by cooperating. But really, right now you're getting your fingerprints all over what could be a key piece of evidence."

"This could be something my wife wrote as a joke," David said. "Probably years ago."

"David," Marie said. Her face was the color and shape of an oblong shell, a shaved almond, a cuttlefish bone on which a parakeet might smooth its beak.

David leaned forward and gently pressed his cheek against hers. It was satisfying, though she felt nothing like an almond. "I understand your concern, but I'm beginning to grow worried for the physical object," he said, cheek to cheek with Marie. "I believe it is within my legal right to keep it."

"I think you should come talk to me sometime," she said, whispering, into his ear.

Chico exhaled through his nose hard enough that David

felt the blast on his face. He took a step back. "It is currently within your legal right," Chico said. "I don't enjoy the fact that you're making that decision, though."

David held the wilted paper aloft. "This object has sentimental value."

"Understood," Chico said. "We're going to compromise."

"Compromise is the evidence of a civil class," Marie said.

Chico produced a pocket camera. "May I?"

David looked first at the camera and then at Marie. He held the threat in his palms, protecting it, while Chico took his picture. Chico put his camera away and handed David a zip-lock sandwich bag from his pocket.

"Keep it in there," he said. "Do you have a stapler?"

David produced one from the junk drawer and Chico stapled the seal with three quick shots.

"We'll head to the salon again. I'm sure we'll find the ones that came by your home."

They both shook David's hand on the way out, and Marie stepped over the pile of frozen clothes on the porch. On their way to the car, Chico touched her arm once above the elbow. "It may not be wise for David to have a private session just yet," he said.

"It would be a safe space for him."

He opened her car door, stepped around the back, and got into the driver's seat. "Maybe soon." As they backed out of the driveway, Chico leveraged his arm against her seat while Marie watched the garage in front of her shrink back into the forest. The garage looked like a second house. She could see one pair of old wooden French doors propped slightly ajar by a substantial wasp's nest that grew between the doors and held them in place.

Inside, David examined the threat. Specks of sugar had fallen to the bottom of the sandwich bag. He thought about the absolute fact that a great number of details had gone unnoticed. He reheated the pot of water, filled his empty cup with sugar. The cup was full to its brim with sugar, and he had to put it in the sink when he poured the hot water in. The sugar sank under the liquid and clouded it, and David stirred it with a small spoon and blew across the surface before sipping the murky, sweet mixture, his lips pursed, his tongue lashing forward. He was a hummingbird. He held the cup at the center of his body, over his heart, wincing as the cup's contents splashed over the lip and onto his fingers.

27

THE YEARS had made Franny literal. It got to the point that when she found something funny, she would say so without laughing. David didn't mind it. He appreciated a literal woman.

Some winter, years before, they had watched a man struggle up the icy hill in front of their home. He plunged silver picks into the ice like an Alpine climber. The man slipped and howled as he fell, digging his pick into his own hand. He slid down the ice in a bloodied mass. Franny smiled, watching. "That was funny," she said. She always asked to see comedies when they went to the movies. He would turn toward her during the funniest parts to find her bobbing her head in agreement. It was as if the characters were explaining the concept of humor to her and she was indicating that she understood. She moved her lips at the movie theater without making a sound.

The only time she would really laugh was when David tried to compare her job to the one he had just been forced to leave. The first time he tried, they were finishing a bottle of wine, standing at the kitchen counter.

"You deal in mystery just as I did," David said. She was

laughing before he began, but he had thought it all out while taking his coffee on the porch earlier that day and was set on sharing. "At your job, you shake a woman's hand, look at her face, she seems fine. But then you get her back, remove her makeup, shine the exam light on her, and you see everything she's hiding. Comedones, age spots, pencil-thin lines. You bring them up and she starts apologizing. 'I know, I should be wearing more sunscreen. I just ran out and forgot to get more.'

"It was exactly the same at my job. I would meet a perfectly nice person, maybe a spectacularly nice person, a minister or a pharmacist, the kind of person I was raised to trust. Then I'd get into his mouth and it would be a disaster. Infection swelling a gum line like a hidden pouch. Trench mouth leaving a gray film on the teeth. Ulcers full of six months' worth of midnight snacks without even a rinse afterward. Back to bed. The guy would say, 'Doc, you gotta understand, I brush my teeth almost every day.' He'd have no reason to lie to me but he would lie. We'd see it all the time."

Franny, pressing her lips together, let out a stifled laugh that startled them both. She set down her wineglass and covered her mouth with both hands. "I'm sorry," she said, snorting. Her face reddened to the ears. "I'm sorry, that's not funny. I'm sorry. I think you're right."

He watched her red ears and felt a lightness in his chest that he hadn't felt since they were dating. From then on, he made a small special effort to compare his old profession to hers. It was so good to see her laugh that he didn't mind. Sometimes she would lean over and hold his hand or even kiss him between peals of laughter. He saved the comparison for special occasions, such as their anniversary.

28

THERE WERE TWO UPSETTING THINGS about the new threat. One item of concern rested in the body of David's father, the other in the body of his mother.

When David and Franny were in their fifth year of marriage, they moved in with his father. This meant moving into David's childhood home, a dark-wooded, many-roomed house on the old side of town. David and Franny had spent the years prior renting their own apartment, but when his father needed help walking from kitchen to basement and eventually from bedroom to bathroom, David found himself spending nights on the sag-springed bed in his first bedroom, and then nights plus weekends, and finally all of the time. He returned to his wife and their apartment, where the landlord wouldn't allow them to put nails in the walls. Their picture frames leaned against the walls from their permanent spots on the floor.

David had spent their savings first paying down the debt of his mother's care, then fighting his malpractice case in court. Without his income, it seemed unlikely that they would be able to hire a home nurse. Franny and David began to consider the monthly expenses they could save by giving up the apartment. Franny mentioned wanting some repairs on the car to fix the heater before winter. The decision to move evolved quickly and came with other benefits. The question of having children was resolved by the presence of David's father, a strange older child, with his stubbed toes and occasional tears and oversize diapers. David's father called them "incontinence products" in the rare instances he mentioned them, saying, "If you are going to the store, I require one box of incontinence products."

The years had worn on the details of the house. Photographs turned yellow and then brown. Upholstered fabric began to show its threads. Spoiled food grew a bacterial fuzz on the dishes piled in the sink. Before he took Franny over to see the place for the first time, David had tried cleaning. He ran three loads of dishes and swept the downstairs and vacuumed the upstairs and dusted picture frames and unscrewed burned-out light-bulbs, wrapping them in newspaper before throwing them away. Franny declared she liked the house and helped him haul bags of garbage out to the curb. David's father watched her warily from his chair. "A busy woman has a plan," he said. In the basement, David showed her the marks on the wall that signified his increasing height, and that of his sister, who was gone before they could make her third mark. Franny asked for the history of the home before David's family had moved in, but he didn't know it. The property was old enough to have a carriage house and a farmer's fence, but it was all in extensive disrepair and offered more nuisance than charm.

It was hard for David to remember how old he was exactly when he and Franny rented a truck and moved in over the course of an afternoon, but he always had a problem with his memory. In fact, he had trouble remembering basic details about his parents, such as their birthdays. He had to go to the drawer by the kitchen door and dig out their old driver's licenses to recall.

David's father sat in his rose-colored recliner and held his journals on his lap long after his vision had regressed to the point of near blindness. To him, living at home meant remaining stubbornly comfortable long after the actual comforts had vanished. After his wife left, David's father had spent many years sitting in his chair. The chair cultivated his scent. The man might read the paper or a book, but more and more often he sat with his hands circled underneath his stomach, looking out the window or more likely looking at the window itself, considering its construction, trying to remember the last time he had had it replaced, how much it had cost at the time, and the conversion of those funds into a modern-day equivalent. He suspected that the window was as few as fifteen and as many as twenty years old. Then he thought at length of the new technologies—those of which he was aware, such as three-paned glass, and those he could only speculate about, such as four-paned glass. He considered the cost of such advanced technology and the resultant energy savings. "A window is a life which presents a life," he said. "A timeline itself, designed to witness an exterior and interior timeline." Thinking in this way, David's father could spend a week in his chair.

In the home for women, David's mother grew happily old. Her room featured a small television mounted in the top corner. She had herself wheeled out to a brightly lit meeting area in the center every morning. Each day, her attendants heard her speaking numbers. At night they wheeled her back to her bedroom, where she slowly changed into her pajamas, climbed into bed, and covered herself with a thin blanket. It was as warm as an incubator in the home for women. She often dreamed of herself as a chicken hatching from an egg.

29

DAVID'S FATHER had been prone to axiom. "Weight is the most important force in your life," he would say, upside down in his inversion machine. David's mother was cooking dinner in the other room, dumping pasta into the strainer, broccoli onto the pasta. "Everything is affected. Everyone succumbs."

His mother tended to make a remark after such statements, but David couldn't remember what she said. Once she was gone, David and his father ate a lot more toast. David's father would regularly make a meal of five pieces of toast. He ate his own toast dry and smeared grape jelly on a single slice for his son. During one such meal he set down the jelly knife, plucked an eyelash off David's cheek, and held it before the boy's face. "You have more intelligence in this eyelash," he said.

"Than what?" David asked, but his father had already left the room, toast in hand.

The man stored pens all over the house. They were taped under desks and tucked over doorframes. He kept them around so he could write down particularly succinct pieces of wisdom or pay the bills while he was taking a bath. He had worked as an accountant and was often writing figures down both sides of a page. Despite never holding a job for more than a few months, he liked to stay informed and involved, to engage his mind.

He valued the knowledge that he gathered during his vast stretches of private time. He liked to make a daily report of the way he spent his hours. He might divide the day into time spent eating toast, sitting in the bathroom, hanging upside down in his inverter, or sitting in his chair, down to the half minute.

After his father died, David read the man's notebooks. There were hundreds of them, lined up carefully on a shelf in the workroom. On the front page of each notebook was written LIVE WITH MEANING in the man's careful block print. It was full of numbers and shorthand, symbols that did not correspond to anything David understood. Columns stretched down the page, unknown symbols on each side. There was a drawing of a window, including what looked like dimensions translated into concentric circles. Behind the line of notebooks David found a box of red pens.

30

WEEKS PASSED. David ate all of the unspoiled perishable foods in the refrigerator and moved on to the pantry, where he found pasta, beans, and a collection of cans of sodium-rich broth, which he heated daily on the stove for his lunch.

The threat that had been placed in a sandwich bag rested in the sun on the kitchen table, in case Chico felt it necessary to come back and have a look. The rest of the threats were collected in the silverware drawer. That afternoon, David had found another to add to the collection. It had been in the pantry, wrapped around a package of spaghetti and secured with a rubber band.

```
I WILL GATHER YOUR OLDEST FRIENDS AT MY HOME
AND WE WILL HAVE A CONVERSATION. YOU WILL
HEAR US TALKING BUT WHEN YOU COME INTO THE
ROOM WE WILL STOP TALKING.
```

David thought about the two boys who had lived down the road. He imagined them sitting there as adults in the living room. Samson would be squeezed into the too-small recliner in the corner of the room, while the other one would sit where David was now, on the couch. He thought of them talking and tried to picture who stood in the center of the room.

He read the threat again and drank his mug of broth until his tongue swelled. He thought of his oldest friends standing with him in someone's father's shed during the time of year when moisture made every surface soft and wooden surfaces a sponge, the three of them sinking into the plywood floor, barely buoyed up by some miracle tension of pulped material. One of them managed to set things on fire despite the high humidity, mostly leaves and sticks and sheets of notebook paper gone so soft in the weather they were like cotton cloth against his matches. Once, the starter of fires lit up the tip of his shoe and danced it back and forth. The other boys laughed before they realized what was happening and then they laughed in a different way, scrambling away, leaving the poor kid to cry and stomp his smoking feet.

Something had to be done. David realized that if he didn't take active steps, it was possible that the threats would continue. He imagined it wouldn't be out of the question to write a letter to his old friends. The letters could be the same beyond their greeting, but David would write them in longhand so that they might feel personalized even though they were identical. It seemed more likely that he would receive a response that way.

It was important to receive a response. If the threats were meant for him, as it seemed they were, it was possible that his friends might know something. Perhaps they had actually had a conversation. David felt good to be considering the possibility of taking active steps.

He dressed without showering, took the newspaper into the living room, and started on the crossword puzzle. The puzzle had a few squares filled out already and he examined the completed squares, frowning, before remembering Dr. Walls sitting at the table. She had figured out the upper-right across and a few three-letter answers scattered throughout, but the puzzle was otherwise blank. David didn't appreciate the kind of person who would answer the simplest questions without considering the whole of the problem. He put the puzzle aside.

The package from the local funeral home made an unattractive centerpiece on the coffee table. It weighed down the permanent display of magazines published with the goal of helping their readership learn about celebrities. It was hard not to see the package, even when it was fully behind his head as he reached toward the bag of Apollonia medals on the highest bookshelf.

There were thirty or forty medals. He usually found more than one a year. When he started leaving the house less and less, Franny showed him how to buy his medals online, and they arrived in sealed bubble wrap containers that lay flat on the kitchen table and gave David no pleasure. Even when Franny threaded one of her best ribbons through it, a red ribbon with velvet on both sides of the fabric, designed to give the wearer the pleasure of velvet at any time, he felt strange admiring it.

He spread his thirty or forty medals out on the table before him. The most expensive was a golden charm with a very clear marking, but he couldn't tell silver from tin, plated gold from solid. The funeral-home package sat at the edge of his eye. He looked up from the medals and his eyes rested on the package.

Whenever she saw smoke on the horizon, Franny took her

keys off their peg by the door. Farmers in the country rid themselves of their brush in the colder months by burning it. The fires sent up plumes that could be seen for miles. Franny might vanish for entire afternoons and return smelling like a campfire. She changed the subject when he asked her where she had been. She started coming home with vegetables she had bought from produce stands along the way. She showed him peas and squash and carrots when he asked why she was missing a shoe. She would roast the vegetables for his dinner and serve them to him in a white bowl. While he ate, she went upstairs to take a shower. Autumn leaves always made him remember the smell of carrots roasting in oil.

David thought of the autumn leaves while observing the Styrofoam container on the coffee table. The shades were drawn over the windows, but he could still hear the noise of people outside. He couldn't tell which of the Apollonia charms was the golden one, as some were gold-filled and others gold-colored and they all looked to be about the same level of quality to David. He picked a silver medal out because he recognized the ribbon from one of Franny's spools. He hung the medal around his neck.

It seemed wrong to put the medals back on the shelf, so he arranged them on the package from the funeral home. It was an attractive memorial. He folded his newspaper, put it in the bag, and threw it into the basement. The bag made a soft sound when it landed at the base of the stairs.

31.

Dear ——,

I hope that you and your family are doing well. It has been a long winter at our house on the hill, and we've been dealing with some issues with the doorknobs in the house. It's nothing a few months won't fix. I know you understand the perils of homeownership.

My apologies that this letter comes too late to be a true Christmas card. I know you appreciate the mystery and tradition of the Christmas season. If I found myself with more daylight, I would be out taking down the lights. Fortunately, there was not enough daylight, so I didn't put any up. I know you understand the perils of light.

I do indeed have a reason for writing you today: I wonder if you've had any occasion within the past five years to speak with another person about me. This could be any other person—my wife, a police officer, a mutual friend—and the exact details of the conversation are not important. The conversation itself is the most important.

If I have your most recent address, you still live in town. I contacted our mutual friend ——; he has responded and is eager to meet with me on the subject. If you would care to join our meeting, please make arrangements to meet at my home on Monday, ——. If you can attend this meeting, I will compensate you five hundred dollars for your trouble.

I look forward to sharing an honest afternoon with my most trusted friends.

Sincerely,

David

32

THE ACT OF CHECKING THE MAIL lost some charm
once records were updated and mail stopped arriving with
Franny's name on it. Also, it was more difficult in the snow.

It had been a warmer winter, which meant more snow than
usual. It was a long forty feet to the mailbox without a shoveled
path. The drifts were deep enough to reach halfway up David's
knee, soaking into his slippers and up the lower leg of his pajama pants, his robe trailing regally behind. The snow shocked
his skin, invading all layers, cupping his heels. He felt that he
had made the last of his intelligent cold-weather clothing decisions many years before, or in a previous life.

Because of his lack of sartorial foresight and the absence of
mail, he made fewer trips to the box, going out once every few
days or weeks to dislodge the catalogs and bills packed inside. He
wore one of Franny's winter hats, which fell over his eyes, making
it so he could see the ground only if he tipped his head back
and to the side. Sometimes pieces of mail were packed so tightly
that removal required finding the most solid object, usually a
magazine, and wrenching it free before the rest would emerge.

One morning the ice climbed the post and moisture seeped in and froze the periodicals completely. David braced himself on the mailbox and reached his ungloved hand inside, coming out with fistfuls of torn bills and circulars that fluttered to the ground as he went back for more. He pulled the majority of it out in one handful, bundled the seeping pile in his arms, and reached down to clean the pieces off the ground. He kicked a stone aside to uncover something that had been wedged underneath. It was a scrap of paper concealed within a Christmas-themed baggie, the type one might use to distribute cookies to neighbors. David wiped the condensation from the baggie onto his jacket and read the page inside:

MY TRUTH WILL BRING ATOMIC SNOW UPON YOUR
SWEET-SMELLING LAMBS AND CHILDREN.

Pocketing the threat, he looked up and down the street. He considered the mail carrier, a man named Edward who wore a safari hat year-round and waved when he saw David standing at the window. David considered the concept of irradiated snowfall and whether it might glow in certain light or darkness. He created an image of what a child might look like if it were also a lamb. The image was of the girls from the salon as lambs with the faces of children, stepping gingerly through his home. One of them pressed her wet nose forward to smell objects while another shit on the rug, then looked at David and spoke words so softly that he was forced to lean close to hear before realizing that the language was not a recognizable dialect of English, if it was in fact English. The words spoken by the child-lamb sounded more like the noise a baby might make to himself while discovering a box of wooden toys crafted to fit into one another, the baby realizing in his discovery that things beyond his control had been created for his amusement, that there was in fact a world beyond the walls of his home, and if the world had created such an object as a wooden star that would fit into a star shape on a board, what other wonders might it hold? In this way, the child is tricked.

David was standing at the end of his driveway. It wasn't snowing, and people walking their pets mistook him for a man wearing a robe by the mailbox. He tucked the bundle of old mail under his arm and was walking alongside the people and their pets before he considered any of it further.

The lack of traction with the road, the way the terrain communicated through the soles, reminded him that he was wearing slippers. He tensed his body, wincing. The slush seeped in. Death made more sense in the winter, in the same way that doing the dishes made more sense in the evening, after a big meal. There was glut in death. David remembered a certain sagging and expanding, a feeling to which he could not assign an image. He created a list of items to help him forget the cold as he walked down the hill.

There was a bus stop at the base of the hill, one he had missed on his previous walks to town. He could imagine Franny riding the bus, a sack of salon tools in her lap underneath a magazine about celebrity home improvement. He imagined her exploring her own perfect tombstone teeth with her pink tongue.

He had no money for the bus. The bus stopped and released a black kid in a puffy jacket and a man with a blanket draped around his body. The two sat together on the bench, ignoring David and each other, waiting for the transfer. The bus driver regarded David's robe and empty hands for a polite moment before snapping the door shut and driving on.

David shifted his bundle of mail from one arm to the other. A thin page advertising pizza fell to the ground, resting wet and looking like a stain or a sore on the sidewalk. "Sorry," David said, stooping to pick up the page. "Does one of you have change? I've lost mine."

The man in the blanket shrugged. He and David regarded the teenager in the jacket, who was at that moment bobbing his head at a tinny noise emanating from the buds in his ears.

"Kids don't know," said the other man. His blanket was secured with a length of rope. "Kids don't respect." He leaned over on the bench and jabbed his finger into the kid's jacket.

"The fuck, man?" the kid said, scowling as a reflex, tucking his thumb under one earbud and popping it out.

David extended his hand. "Do you have a couple quarters for the bus?"

The two ignored him.

"The fuck you say," said the guy in the blanket. He jerked his head down and back as if he was trying to physically navigate the words. "The fuck, you say."

"Sorry," David said to the kid. "I didn't have any quarters."

The kid retained the scowl and dug in his pocket for the dollar and twenty-five cents. "Here, man," he said, leaning to deposit the money into David's hand. David found a forty-cent coupon for laundry detergent in his bundle of mail. He extracted the page and offered it to the kid, who held up one hand to block the transaction.

"The fuck you say," said the other man, grasping a piece of his blanket and tugging it tighter over his legs. David thought about how nice it would feel to be draped in a blanket at that moment. It had begun to snow. The blanket man was looking right at the kid, who had replaced his earbuds and was bobbing again, pressing the miniature keys of a phone he had produced from his pocket.

"Kids ignore you these days," said the man. "Ten years ago this kid and I would have had a nice call-and-response, a pleasant altercation. We would have talked, you know? Like human beings need to talk? To be all right? Now kids ignore you. Back then more people were familiar with the concept of jazz." He tightened his cord and leaned back into his side of the bench. It looked like he went to sleep immediately, but then he opened one eye and directed it toward David. "You familiar with the concept of jazz?"

"They've got all this gear now," David said. He had never purchased a cellular phone. The weighty molded plastic of the real telephone cupped too nicely in his hand to give it up. Against his ear it felt like an actual method of communication. He had used Franny's cell phone once, and it felt as if he was speaking into a potato chip. He didn't want the daily experience. It was hard enough adjusting to the digital answering machine Franny had set up on the landline.

The blanket man closed his eye. "I don't like the color of his jeans or the content of his character," he said. "I know this is sounding real 'kids these days,' but man, kids these days, you know? These guys don't even talk to their girlfriends anymore. They'll sit and send them text messages all damn day, but the instant this gorgeous girl walks in and alights next to him like a thick-waist bird of paradise, the guy's on the damn phone sending the text message. Girl's all batting the phone outta his hand,

'Come on, Regis,' got that sweet little pout on. Regis wants to know the score of some damn game that'll still be there when he's done laying hands on this girl. Kids these days have no concept of jazz."

The bus rounded the corner and shuddered to a stop before them. The doors opened and the bus hissed and lowered, coming to an easy angle with the curb. The man with the blanket stood and shuffled on first, while David waited behind and then followed. The silent kid looked up at the number on the side of the bus and back down to his phone.

33

FRANNY had always been overconcerned with her small flaws, the spider veins sprouting like thin roots from the curves of her nostrils. She covered her face daily with thick creams and powders that caused her forehead and cheeks to resemble a tanned volleyball. Her complexion cracked when she spoke. In part because of the attention Franny brought to it, David remembered his wife's face as easily as he forgot the town where they had lived. The town was composed of a main road with branching side streets and a few small shops surrounding the police station, where Detective Chico was likely sitting at his desk, regarding a set of photographs he had taken of David's home. Between a sandwich shop and the furniture outlet was a long, thin split in the tanned brick with what looked like scorch marks emerging from either side. His old dental office had been on the north side of town, and he avoided walking past it.

He had to circle around the town square twice before he found Franny's salon. Inside, the place was softly lit. Its building had previously housed a pool hall in one large room. The new owner built thick walls that stretched up eight feet before terminating in open space. It gave the whole thing the look of a television studio. As he approached the reception desk, David thought he caught a glimpse of boom mic rigging over the far wall.

The girl behind the desk had her black hair pulled up in the same wrapped style that Franny had always worn to work. A tattoo of a bear on its hind legs dominated the center of her chest, its haunches nestled in the cleavage of her tank top.

"Do you have an appointment?" she asked her computer. The computer did not respond, and she looked at David. "Sir?"

"Sorry," he said. "Yes, I don't have an appointment. I'm sorry. No." He saw that she was looking at him hard, and he realized he was still carrying the bundle of junk mail. He tried to compress it in his arms.

"You don't have an appointment?"

"I'm here to see my wife," he said. He thought of Franny applying liniments to a face behind one of the half walls. "She's not here, I mean. I'm here to see about her."

The tattooed girl frowned. "Does your wife have an appointment?"

"My wife, Franny."

The girl squinted at David in a confused way that still managed to suggest that he was an idiot. She leaned forward, observing his armful of mail. "You mean Frances?" she asked. She smelled clean and chemical, like a plastic bag.

David leaned in as well. "Did you come to my house the other day?" he asked.

The girl reared back and the bear reared with her. David gripped the reception desk, concerned that one or the other might strike.

"Let me get my manager," the girl said. She tossed the phone toward its charging base, and David could still hear the beep-beep of a disconnect alert as she walked into the back room. With a tentative finger, he corrected the phone in its dock. It was a harmless phone, of course. The phone was harmless.

Franny had moved through the rooms and doors of their home for years, but David felt something special standing there in this new place. It was a place he had never entered but one she knew well, and this gave everything a glowing outline of magic. Perhaps she had touched that very phone, gripped that doorknob, swept that floor. Surely she wore one of the shared black aprons to match the rest of the staff. Maybe, over the course of many years, she had worn all of the aprons. David felt like a tourist in the salon, standing in awe of each invisible attraction. He had just walked behind the reception desk when a short woman with shocking blonded hair emerged from the back room and put her hand on his arm. She looked the same, though he hadn't seen her in years. "Aileen," he said.

"I'm so sorry for your loss."

Closer up, David saw that Aileen wore the same poreless mask that Franny had layered on every morning. He placed these two women in the same tribe, not old yet but older than the tattooed girls working around them. Aileen and Franny spent all day performing chemical peels on the curled rinds of aging skin, ministering to younger women just starting to understand the weakness and betrayal of the skin organ and seeking a solution in a burning enzyme. Franny had given him a chemical peel once, and he was aware of his skin screaming at the intrusion.

"It's been so long," Aileen said. She was holding two cups of water and offered David one. He accepted it, tucking the junk mail into his pocket, and she placed the other cup on the reception counter. "Frances was one of my closest friends," she said.

"Then I'm sorry for your loss as well," he said.

"Please, have some water."

He brought the cup to his lips. A pond smell in the liquid stopped him from drinking. He imagined hidden microbes. "I'm not too thirsty," he said. He put the cup on the counter. "Thank you, though."

She picked the cup up and handed it to him again. "Thirst is your body warning you of dehydration."

"I'm fine," he said. "Thank you. I just drank some water at my home."

"It's important to drink when you're not thirsty." She touched his hand with her hands. They held the cup together. She lifted her hands up slightly, guiding the liquid toward his mouth.

"I've really had a lot of water already," he said. "Thank you, though."

Aileen regarded him with a smiling kind of distrust and released his hand. She turned and gestured toward the reception area with two open arms. "I've been throwing myself into updates," she said. "I'll give you the tour."

He followed Aileen down the hall. The owner was a largely absent businessman from out of town who mostly franchised fast-food chains but had a soft spot for the beauty trade. He turned the daily hassles of running the place over to his senior attendants, which meant that in addition to their aesthetician duties, Franny had managed the stylists and Aileen enjoyed the privileges of decor and arrangement.

The salon waiting room was cluttered with useless delicate

things. An ornate bar, ridiculously mirrored, held a full tea service, cookies and jams, a sleek black pitcher of lukewarm coffee. The tinkling beads of a miniature crystal chandelier caressed David's forehead. The room seemed to be three feet too small from all sides, giving it the feeling of progressing in an orderly collapse toward the center. He imagined Franny's head grazing the low ceiling. She would have to stoop to exit the room, and he thought of her emerging on the other side, smiling.

Aileen picked up the pitcher and shook it before placing it back on its tray. "The girls should refill this," she said. "I decorated this whole room with pieces I found from estate sales. Frances loved it."

David hummed a low response, and Aileen led the way to the salon area, equally appointed. Before he left the room, he placed the cup of water on the mirrored bar.

Stylists picked their tools from painted vintage tables as clients regarded themselves in a trio of heavy gilt mirrors installed over each station. The walls and concrete floor were stained a mahogany red. David watched the clients receiving scalp massages. Their bodies were wrapped in thin black robes. They smiled fatuously under the stroking of expert fingers.

He saw that one of these smiling women was Marie Walls, the woman who had sat at his table and completed a portion of his crossword puzzle while telling him about how he should feel. A girl was massaging her hands with a thick cream.

"Marie," David said. "How are you?"

At the first sign of a third-party conversation, Aileen turned without further remark and made a circle of the salon floor, observing the stylists with her hands on her hips.

"Hang on, I can't see you too well," Marie said. "Come closer."

He approached her chair, leaned in. "Hello, David. I'm perfect at the moment. There's nothing like a rub, you know?"

"It looks nice."

Marie narrowed her eyes to look at Aileen, who was plucking at a foil wrap. "Are you here for a haircut?" she asked David.

"I'm getting the tour. My wife worked here."

"And how are you feeling?" she asked, examining her hand.

David tried to focus on the history of his emotions. All he remembered was the feeling of standing in the other room, the chandelier's crystals against his forehead. "Fancy," he said.

"You should come to my office and have a talk with me sometime. I'd be willing to meet with you free of charge. That's a rare privilege I've extended to you."

"That is kind."

The girl moved from Marie's hands and went to work massaging her scalp. Marie groaned. "Well," she said, gripping the arms of the chair and closing her eyes. "We do what we can."

Aileen returned with a pair of scissors. "These young girls," she said.

34.

PHOTOGRAPHS of photographs tend to take on a strange quality of their own, independent of the subject they try to capture. The glass of the photo's frame and the glass of the camera lens together offer an extra layer between the item and the capturing device, giving the air between them a darker quality. Of course, any dust on the picture frame or intruding natural light can further degrade the image. The resulting picture represents the murky edges, facial expressions blurred and unclear. The individuals in the frame are difficult to separate from the elements of scenery.

Detective Chico enjoyed the imperfections of the images in front of him. He had taken pictures of a few of the snapshots he found in frames on the kitchen counter while David was busy digging the threat out of its sugar bag. He didn't want to bother the man or go to the unnecessary trouble of confiscating the pictures themselves.

It was a quiet town, and Chico's area of expertise rarely extended past the boundaries of underage drinking and traffic stops. The last time the office had gotten worked up, it was because a semi driver rolled over the boot of one of the sheriff's patrol. The steel-toed reinforcement had bent but not broken over the man's foot and the driver stopped, expressed his regret, and later sent an unnecessary but appreciated formal letter of apology to the entire office. "I am a Respecter of our Nation's legal enforcement," the letter began.

Such a mystery as David's was nearly new ground for Chico, who had enjoyed forty years without so much as a crossing guard fatality. He had stood at the scene of the potential crime, watching a man pull a threatening note from a bag of sugar, and felt the importance of his surroundings.

The detective had observed his surroundings with the interest of a man who had never truly been asked to do his job in years. He recalled his training. He took photographs and memorized the layout of the space in the event that he would have to reenter under duress.

Chico saw himself as a helpful spirit. He tried to give people what they needed, within the guidelines of legality. When the woman arrived asking for a random selection of old clothes from his evidence lockup, he was happy to oblige. There were clothes in there thirty or forty years old, the cases closed. The clothes would have been incinerated otherwise. The woman was doing him a favor, in a way. When she returned to ask him to give her nephew some work he obliged her, even when he learned that the boy was too young for a traditional internship.

It was important to give people what they needed. Sometimes, a woman needed to go to jail, or a man needed to be chased in a parking garage. In his years of service Chico had learned that people tended to know what they needed, even if they didn't know how to ask for it.

The pictures were exactly the kind that Chico would expect to find on a kitchen countertop. There was a shot of the man and his wife in front of the town's embarrassingly nondescript city hall, each experiencing formal wear in individually awkward ways, the woman wilting over her husband, a bouquet of flowers spread over her fist like stained lace. Another picture featured an older couple, presumably a set of parents, posing on the Great Wall of China. The detective looked closer and saw that it was only a representation of the Great Wall blown up to cover a concrete slab behind them. A child in the corner of the frame crouched to collect peanuts from a quarter candy machine. The woman in the picture looked familiar, and Chico, who never could forget a face, spent some time frowning at the image before he remembered her from the trial.

It was six long months' worth of trial, her lawyer flown in from Chicago. He was a broad-shouldered man who managed to physically intimidate the judge from across the chamber. The lawyer spoke of the disastrous effects of the powerful and powerfully in-vogue teratogen the grieving mother had ingested while innocently pregnant. Pregnancy was one of the world's most innocent conditions, the lawyer claimed, resting his hand on the mother's shoulder while she sobbed. It all added up to six months of trial delays and jury recasts and that city lawyer's patient explanation and re-explanation of what a mother could and couldn't do under duress, what the psychological texts stated, what that might prove, his expert witnesses consulting their years of knowledge to bolster the fact that a mother who had the power to end a child she had viewed as a living defect was not a mother at all, but rather a creature acting under the influence of insanity. Chico took the stand again and again to perform his dull role of explaining the scene as he saw it, the medics not bothering with the heavier equipment once they saw the child's bloat in the water, the absence of a pulse. Chico sometimes sat in the gallery during his lunch break and watched how easy it was for the court's hands to be tied by procedure. He thought of how he had been offered a position in Columbus, how glad he was in hindsight that he hadn't taken it, watching how the system stuttered. He imagined the broad-shouldered lawyer carrying the judge like a child in his arms.

The third picture Chico had found in the house was of the woman from city hall, the wife, the decedent, standing with another woman. The decedent was holding an armful of flowers and wearing a cap and gown, a graduation photo. She was grinning, exposing a wide expanse of teeth. The other woman held up a fistful of black combs. Chico observed the images carefully. Understanding them each individually would help him gain a fuller understanding of the world he was intruding upon. He did feel like an intruder, looking at these other people's photographs. Still, he looked, taking in their details.

35

DAVID SOMETIMES MISSED HIS PATIENTS. He thought of his old friend Samson's plaque layer, listening to his lies about brushing as the hygienist's floss nicked eruptions of rot-stenched blood. The gums had begun to loosen and peel from his teeth like pages in a book, and still Samson said yes, brushing every day, yes, flossing after meals, why there's floss in the truck, yes of course.

The behavior of each new patient could never be predicted. Some young children would come in and immediately relax in the big chair. Others clung to their mothers and screamed while David darted into their mouths with his periodontal probe. Some mothers would cry, working their children up even more. Children were usually sensitive enough that a parent unconsciously gripping them could put them off dentistry for the rest of their lives. He saw the impulse to squirm and cry in adults as well, though all but the very old tended to keep calm. David's knowledge and preferences of parenting techniques extended to the boundary of his examination room.

There were the older girls and boys, the teenagers. They arrived at the office without their mothers, holding their parents' insurance cards and blank checks. When there were two teenagers in the waiting room at once, the whole building could sense the tension. Nobody could handle it. His receptionist would close the glass partition and go out back for a smoke. In the examination room, David prodded their teenage mouths and tried to figure the age his baby sister would be at that moment, had she survived.

There were men and women who did care for their teeth well and nevertheless had problems. He coaxed weak enamel from talonid surfaces, the grinding flat of the tooth giving way to pre-cavity areas. David felt the problems in a tooth even before the tooth made its problems known to its owner, before the ache in a bite of ice cream, the stinging intake of winter air. He could graze the tooth and feel something lurking.

What had made David a good dentist—an excellent dentist, in his opinion—was his keen ability to sense weakness prior to its development. A patient would come in without tooth pain, talking about a football game, and be surprised to learn that a cavity needed to be drilled and filled. David would point to the darkening patches on the X-ray, still subtle even there, as if the damage was being viewed from under a rippling layer of fluid. A lesser dentist might not even be able to spot it. The patient would frown at the image but relent, knowing precisely as much as he did before but trusting David's professional opinion. The patient might wince through the Xylocaine but would hold as still as a sleeping dog while the dentin was breached and burred, Dycal installed to obliterate the possibility of a return, a white resin filler approximating the shape and texture of a tooth so closely it made David wish for his patients' sake that the entire procedure could be performed without their knowledge, that they could come in unknowing and leave unknowingly improved. It seemed a kindness to improve upon an individual without his knowledge. David didn't understand why anyone might see otherwise, particularly not the dental board of Ohio, composed as it was of former dentists and medical administrators who had presumably once felt the same protective urge for their patients, a nurturing urge they might feel for their families.

36

DAVID once saw Franny apply five layers of makeup to her lips. She lined them first with a pencil and then applied lipstick, some kind of powder, lipstick again, and then another tube that also looked like lipstick but was perhaps not lipstick. He had tried to kiss her afterward but she held her hands over her mouth.

The salon's facial treatment room was dimly lit. Scented oils in bottles lined the wall. The room smelled so strongly of Franny that David had to take a seat on the rolling chair beside the bed. It felt better to be sitting on the chair. The room didn't spin so much as it rocked slightly, unevenly, a cradle guided by a distracted hand. David wondered if Aileen would notice if he put his face against the wall.

"Here's where she spent most of the day," Aileen said. "Extractions, peels, facial massages, oil treatments, waxing." She laid down her scissors and counted off the list on her fingers. "She was the best in the local business, besides me."

"Ha," David said. He rolled backward on the chair, away from her and toward the wall.

"David, I'm so glad you came to see us today. I've wanted to talk to you ever since it happened. I have so many questions. Could you answer some of my questions?"

"I'll try," David said. He dispensed a small amount of lotion into his hand and rubbed his palms together. The lotion lathered, and he realized that it was soap. "I have some confusion," he said. "It's been difficult to sort things out."

"Is it true that the police have been by the house?"

Tea candles were burning in misshapen sand-colored bowls. David rested his wrists on his knees, his soapy hands palms up. He put his forehead against the wall and then the side of his face. He closed his eyes. "They want to talk about what I know," he said. "I'm always disappointing them. I don't know anything."

"You don't know what happened at all?" she asked. "Where did you put your water?"

"Did you send some women from the salon to my home?"

"Some girls?"

"Some women, some girls. A group of them arrived a few days ago and said they had been sent to cut my hair. They were very kind and helpful. One of them cut my toenails."

"Some girls," Aileen said. She took a deep breath in and looked at the door. She was silent for long enough that he thought she hadn't heard part of the question. "A group of girls. Yes, I sent over a group of girls from the salon. I thought it might make you feel better."

"Thank you, it did."

"I was worried you would find it too difficult."

"Not at all," he said. He wanted to rinse off his hands in the room's sink but didn't want to seem insensitive. "It was nice to see people, and they were such nice girls. I'd like to pay them for their services."

Aileen waved off the suggestion. "Think nothing of it, David. It's the least we can do to help. We've all been so worried about you, and so curious."

"I understand that."

"Frances was one of my closest friends."

"I know."

"It's easy to be curious."

"I know that."

"I've gathered some of her personal effects." She pulled a box out from under the treatment sink and handed it to David. "I thought you might like to have them."

The box was closed and David wanted to keep it that way. He felt that opening the box would release Franny's ghost, that life after the box had been opened would make a distinct shift to a new form, a sugar cube dissolving in a saucer of tea, a hair trimmed from a nose. The hair, the nose, each altered forever. Aileen was watching him with a slight frown. He tucked one finger under the cardboard edge and opened it up. It looked to be the contents of a locker. There was an empty folder, a half-crushed package of chips, eight dollars in crumpled bills. Her aesthetician license, featuring a photo booth–size Franny grimacing through makeup. A folded apron lined the box. David searched the apron pocket, thinking about the times his wife had put her hands there. He found a paper scrap that could have come from a fortune cookie:

TRY TO KISS ME. SEE WHAT HAPPENS TO YOUR LIPS.

Aileen was watching him. Her lips seemed to have been injected with a chemical designed to increase their volume. David had heard about this type of treatment from his wife. The chemical made her lips look smooth and unreal, as if she had thoughtlessly mouthed a piece of slick plastic until it fused to her skin. David thought of the clear plastic spreaders he put in his patients' mouths before X-rays, how the piece curled their lips into animal grimaces. He thought of his own lips, which felt dry and seemed to be peeling off in ribbons, a ticker-tape parade on his face.

"If you ever need my help, you shouldn't hesitate," Aileen said through the protrusion on her face, handing him her card.

He accepted it with the threat fortune in his palm.

"Think of me as your listening ear," she said. Her lips seemed more capable of listening than her ears, which were masked behind a perfect shelf of platinum dyed hair.

He thought of a wet slit in her lips opening to reveal an inner ear, prehensile, protected by the mass around it. Her lip's inner ear would be prepared to listen in the precise way that inner ears are able to listen.

David stopped by the decorated waiting room before he left. Above the coffee station, a palm-size painting of a girl in a dress caught his attention. The girl's dress was flounced and dotted with pink and black. She carried a tiny umbrella in her gloved hands and smiled in a compelling way that caused David to lean even closer to her face. He leaned very close.

She's lying, the girl said.

"Well, yes." The force of his whispered breath close to her pushed the curls back from the girl's face.

It is time to go home. You won't like what you find there. The girl rustled the umbrella, releasing crystal droplets. The drops sank into her dress where they landed. The girl's lips were so tiny that they must have been painted on with a single brush bristle bound to a toothpick with a single hair.

David saw a corner of something sticking out between the frame and the wall. He shifted the box of Franny's things to one arm and worked the paper out from behind the frame. The frame was delicate and shivered against his movements as he unstuck the paper. The page was a thin receipt from the frame shop, featuring Franny's dark signature. David tucked it into the box and held it protectively against his stomach as he left.

37

ON THE WAY TO THE BUS STOP, he picked up pears and bread from the grocery store, paying with Franny's eight dollars from the cardboard box, which he held in both hands. He made pleasant conversation with the cashier about eating pears in the winter. The cashier said that the pears came from New Mexico and that she had never been to New Mexico but imagined it was nice.

He carried the pears in a paper bag tucked into the box and navigated the icy walk toward his home. As he got close, he saw a van parked out front. A few people took photographs and stepped carefully across the snowy drive. His first thought was that they were police, but he saw people of all ages, adults and children. Everyone was wearing overstuffed coats and new boots and hats. They were tourists.

"What are you doing here?" David asked a man aiming a silver wafer of a camera at his front door.

"This is the house," the man said. "Where It Happened."

David felt as if he was reading titles on a bookshelf. "Where What Happened?"

"That Poor Woman." The man reviewed the shots on his wafer.

"Everything Is Dead, but It's Still Kind of Nice," said a woman observing the frozen house plants on the porch.

Two children chased each other around the mailbox and up the driveway. They were saddled with heavy canvas bags that looked to be full of newspapers. "Say You're Sorry," one called out to the other. "I Never Will," the other called back.

"I Have to Leave Here," David said. "You People Are Driving Me Insane." He couldn't leave. He wanted to put the box of Franny's personal effects in a safe place inside the house and eat one of the pears. The tourists were treating the whole house as if it were a personal effect. The two children had taken a brief pause from chasing each other to stand at the shrubs under the windows and crush the leaves' ice pockets between their knit-gloved fingers. A woman who was presumably their mother saw David looking at them and walked behind the house without comment.

David approached a woman sitting with her back to the van, drawing the front porch on a large sketch pad spread out over her lap. "How many of you are there?" he asked.

"Ten," the woman said. "Were you the husband?"

"Was I the husband," David said.

The woman squinted. "We're not going inside," she said. "We wouldn't go in there. This whole thing has been on the news, that's all."

"What has?"

"The case, the warrant." She picked a piece of charcoal from a sheet of wax paper on her lap and squinted at the porch. Her right hand was blackened by the coal, and flakes of it dotted her blouse. He craned his neck to observe her sketch and saw that her rendering of the porch resembled a buffet counter.

"Stop that," he said.

"Stop what?"

"You're drawing my front porch."

"They're looking into things, you know. They are calling this a case of interest."

A man opened the passenger door of the van and produced a brown bag lunch. David saw a child asleep on a stack of newspapers inside the van. The man leaned against the van and unwrapped a candy bar.

"We drove an hour to come see it," the woman said. She added a sneeze guard to the buffet.

"Hour and a half," the man said, unwrapping his candy bar and taking a bite.

"There's a warrant?" David said. "To arrest someone?"

She smudged the cashier station with her thumb, squinting up at the house for reference. "It's to search the place, I think. I don't know, maybe it's an arrest thing too. I hadn't heard all of it."

"This is all news to me."

"And you're news to us. Your picture is all over the place. It's file footage from when you were last in the news, after some accident in the park. Can you believe how time progresses? You look a bit older now."

David thought of the accident in the park. He had been shocked by a hanging power line while his mother was talking to a friend. He hardly remembered any of it, but in the following years he had become the example case for parents to teach their children to avoid all manner of unknown danger. "I was five," he said.

"Time flies"—she tapped the pad—"when we're having fun. I'm trying to have the most fun with the time I have. You know, I used to work as a large-animal vet, but today I'm an artist by choice. My best paintings come from places with a wealth of emotional . . . emotional"—she looked to the man and then to the sky and then to David again—"*currency*. A wealth, or at least a favorable exchange rate. You get the concept. When I saw this on the news I just knew it was time to start a new piece. Then all I needed to do was rent a van and spread the word."

The man crumpled the candy wrapper and put it in his paper bag. "Drove a full hour and a half," he said. "Wouldn't believe the snow right outside town. We're simple folk."

"You would not believe how simple we are," said the woman.

"That's a good thing," said the man.

"You would not believe how good it is."

The man spit into the road. "I get the sense there's not a lot he would believe."

"I believe that there are trespassers on my lawn," David said.

"So call the police," said the man. He stuffed the wax paper from his sandwich into the front pocket of his jeans. "They won't need directions."

A child ran by with a messenger bag full of bundled newspapers.

"They could be here in thirty minutes or less," the woman said. "Like a pizza."

"Faster than a pizza," said the man.

The woman had begun to sketch a child standing in front of the house. The child was holding a pane of window glass like a tray. David saw other children fighting over more glass against the garage door. Children who looked too young to be walking staggered back under the fragile weight of their find. He didn't recognize the glass and didn't know how it had come to rest against his garage door. It looked like a windowpane, but he didn't see the frames or brackets. He thought for a moment that the glass was sheets of ice but saw that the children were holding it with their bare hands.

"You'll cut yourself," he said, walking toward the child by the porch, walking faster, jogging. The child saw David approaching and ran wordlessly, arms spread, fingers clutching the edges of the glass.

David considered chasing the child. He felt watched by the man and woman by the van. "Control your children!" he called out. The children by the glass looked back, but the adults didn't seem to hear. A pair of women emerged from the woods, arms locked around a substantial log. "Please leave!" he shouted. "I am calling the police." The women walked by without hearing and loaded the log into the back of a four-door sedan. David headed for the house. He stepped to the side to avoid an old woman prying a souvenir shard from the porch rail. He unlocked the front door and locked it behind him.

He put the pears on the kitchen counter with Franny's box from work. Then he threw the junk mail and the paper bag from the grocery into the basement. The slick circulars stuck to the stairs.

38

THERE WAS A DIFFERENCE in the way the air felt on David's face and neck. Someone had been inside the house.

The intruder was an expert tracker. In the kitchen, the tracker had opened the refrigerator door and examined the contents. He or she had moved the jar of mustard a half inch to the left. David wondered if anything had been found there.

The threats were still in the silverware drawer, curled up against the spoons. The tracker could have found them and recorded their contents. David imagined the faceless tracker crouched over them, transcribing their contents into a notebook and then gathering them carefully, putting the sugar threat back into its plastic baggie, realigning the staples perfectly. David placed the stapled baggie in another baggie. Somewhere out there, he knew, there was an advertising salesperson who had updated "bag" to become "baggie" to make it more appealing to the baggie-buying class, which had once included David's wife.

Franny's cardboard box was on the kitchen counter. The edges had lost their shape when he crushed them against his chest on the trip home. He couldn't determine the age of Franny's aesthetician's license photo but decided it was about ten years old, judging by her hairstyle. He folded it once and put it in his robe pocket. He took a closer look at the receipt that had been taped behind the frame and found words typed over the page:

HOBBY HOUSE
1703 N. DARLING ST.

| TERMINAL ID | 79594746 |
| MERCHANT # | 43013300 |

CASH
SALE

| I WILL LOCK YOU IN A ROOM MUCH LIKE YOUR OWN UNTIL IT BEGINS TO FILL WITH WATER. PICTURE FRAME | $3.95 |

TAX	$0.26
TOTAL PAID	$5.00
CHANGE	$0.79

HAVE A NICE DAY

David thought of Franny paying for a threat with a five-dollar bill and receiving seventy-nine cents in return. He thought of her pink wallet with the clasp, and he slipped the receipt into the sandwich bag with the other threat and put it into his pocket with Franny's aesthetician's license.

It seemed best that he not make any sudden moves that

might alert the tracker, in case he or she was still watching. He boiled water, stirred cinnamon into the pot, poured the mixture into a mug, and took it to check the rest of the house.

Whoever had been there went upstairs as well. The tracker had taken fiber samples from the carpet where it began again at the top of the stairs. David could tell that things had been disturbed.

Items from the bathroom counter had been collected. One of Franny's travel-size bottles of hair product was open in the sink, leaking down the drain. David wished he had photographed the area before leaving the house. The water in his mug bloated the cinnamon. David watched the water rolling over the dark texture of the spice. He tipped back the cup and allowed the wet lump of cinnamon to roll into his mouth. It was like eating a hot slug.

"David," someone called from downstairs. The slug quit its progression down David's throat. He coughed to dislodge it, coughed again, swallowed.

"David? Are you up there?" asked the voice. It was a man's voice, and one David didn't recognize. Someone had been in the house all along. David thought of the dumb fact of it as he walked to the stairwell and leaned around the corner.

A balding man stood at the base of the stairs. He wore a brown sweater over a collared shirt and tie, which made him look very much like David's middle school vice principal. The man had one hand on the staircase rail and the other resting protectively on his stomach.

"David, it's Ted," the man said at the same moment that David realized it was Ted, his old friend Ted, the one who started fires, whose parents allowed him to prop a wide board over the curb at his house so Ted and David and Samson could speed down and into the street on their bicycles.

"Ted. You came."

"Sorry, we let ourselves in. The back door was open. We had to chase some woman with a camera out of the kitchen. Hey, what's going on here?"

Samson came forward to stand next to Ted at the base of the stairs. "Those people have been there for hours," he said. "We figured they didn't belong. Someone broke the window over your kitchen table. I took it off the tracks for you."

"Thanks, Samson. How are you?"

"You'll need to get some plywood to patch it up," Samson said. "I looked for some in the garage, but there was a woman in there who told me to get out."

"We've been here a while too," Ted said. He was holding a folded newspaper.

"At least we were invited," said Samson.

"What's going on?" David asked.

"Asked you that." Ted shrugged. "Apparently, your house was on the news. I missed it."

"So those are people who watch the news," Samson said. "I've always wondered what they look like."

"Too much happening to watch the news," Ted said. "It's too depressing."

"They seemed like nice enough people," Samson said.

"A murder here, a suicide there," said Ted. "Who can take it? Nurses at the trauma ward all, 'Somebody else died. Call the paper.'"

"But they seemed real nice," Samson said.

"It's strange how many people could come out on a Tuesday afternoon," David said. "Why would they all take off work, pull their kids out of school?"

"It's Sunday," Ted said. "Church crowd."

David considered the progression of days.

"I fixed that dripper in your bathroom," Samson said. "Thing needed a new washer; I had one in the truck. Nothing better to do. You should get a television."

"I got your note in the mail," Ted said. "Then Samson called and we figured we'd come over right away."

"A friend in need," Samson said.

"Why don't you come on down? We're having some beers in the sitting room."

Samson, who had been holding his beer at his waist, brought it up and took a drink. "Been too long," he said, resting his hand on his belly, rubbing the spot. David came down the stairs and accepted a beer from Ted. The tourists outside were starting to lose interest in the house. A couple took off, walking up the street with their cameras. David watched them leave from the front window.

The men drank their beers. "One of those kids sold me a paper," Ted said. "Missing a sports section, though. Strange people for strange times. I'll tell you, I've never seen so many strange people come into the dealership. Used to be, we'd get a wild-eyed man come in talking about buying a car, we'd call the police before he could kick a single tire. These days, it's all you see. Man yelling on prices while his woman stands outside with the kids. It's getting harder to part a fool and his money, or maybe they're all fools now."

"I come to houses where the pipes are all messed up," Samson said. "These guys try to fix it themselves. They get online and read about it. The DIY guys aren't new, but it's the consistency of it these days. A woman last week broke the bowl clean in half trying to pry out her kid's toy with a crowbar. She actually had a crowbar in there." He looked at David. "Ever put a crowbar in a toilet?"

"No," David said.

"You're all right," Samson said.

"How long has it been?" said Ted. "Millie's nearly nine now, and I know you haven't been over since she was a baby."

"Nine years," said David.

"Tell you, that girl's the light of my life."

"There's a special place in heaven reserved for the fathers of girls," Samson said.

"Thanks, Sam."

"A crowbar. Incredible. Sometimes I want to fix plumbing problems and keep them from becoming a real nightmare, you know? I can see something's falling apart. I'm a professional."

"I know exactly what you mean," said David. The beer was cold in his hand. He couldn't remember the last time he'd had a beer. "Thanks for coming, guys."

"What are friends for?" Ted said, picking up the beer. "I'm gonna throw these in the fridge."

"It's been so long," David said after Ted had gone. "And with all this happening."

"With all what happening?"

"Franny, you know. Franny's accident."

Samson leaned forward. "Franny had an accident?" he said. "When?"

"Well, yes. A few weeks ago. Or months," he said. "Maybe six months ago. Maybe a year."

"Is she all right?"

"I thought you might have seen it on the news."

"She didn't mention anything."

"Who didn't?"

"Franny didn't. What happened?"

He felt like a propped-up cardboard cutout of a man. "When did you talk to her?"

"Not too long ago. I drove by the house, had a job up the street."

"You're mistaken," David said, holding his hand against the buzzing in his ear.

"I know Franny. Tall woman, big features. Brown hair down to the middle of her back." He measured the spot on his own back where her hair would fall if it was on his head. The buzzing grew louder. "She answered when I called her name. This wasn't too long ago."

"She was mistaken," David said. "You were mistaken. It was a coincidence. Common name."

Samson peeled at the label of his empty beer. "Did you think she'd run off somewhere?"

Ted came back into the room, grasped the arm of the chair, and lowered himself. When the full weight of his body hit the chair, a mechanical pencil dropped to the floor. Only David saw the motion. The double-sided tape ringing the pencil was coated with fuzz from the underside of the chair. "Who's gone?" Ted asked.

"I saw your wife, David," Samson said.

"Franny?" Ted sank his chin into his neck, as if the idea had tapped him on the forehead.

"Now that girl's a tall drink," Samson said.

"Such a good girl," said Ted. "We sure wish you two would come by more often."

David set his beer on the carpet, keeping it upright with an extended finger. He imagined Franny among the tourists, confused. The buzzing grew even louder, a machine whir in his ears, but it seemed as if his friends couldn't hear it. It was important in that moment to have a fruitful conversation.

"What did she say to you when you talked?" he asked.

Samson frowned. "You two fighting?"

"Did she say we were?"

"I mean, it all depends on context," Ted said. "Everything is different if you two are fighting. She could say 'Oh, he's working on the doghouse,' and if you're not fighting, then you're actually working on a doghouse, but if you're fighting, then she's trying to say something in code, see?"

"We don't own a dog."

"It's code."

"An expression," said Samson. "That's what he's saying."

"You should get a cell phone," Ted said.

David clapped his hands over his ears, boxing them. The buzzing stopped. He exhaled.

"Sorry, man," said Ted.

"Maybe you could tell us what she told you exactly," David said. "We can all figure out the context together."

"They were fighting," Samson said. "Listen. This wasn't too long ago. When I saw her, I got out of the truck and she was standing in front of the house. She was smiling real big too, now that I think about it. It was noticeable because I never saw the girl smile, not even in those early days. But there she was, smiling and playing with the buttons on her jacket like a little one. I tried to give her a hug but she took a step back, and I remembered"—he paused—"I remembered how she is. I asked her what she was up to and she shrugged, said she wasn't up to nothing, and pointed at the house. It seemed like it hurt to talk, and when I asked her if she'd been sick she kind of nodded and held her throat.

"She did say one strange thing," Samson went on. "I asked if you were around, if maybe I could come in and warm up. My job wasn't for a few hours at least. I wasn't wearing my boots, and the cold was starting to get to me, you know. Doctor says I should eat more fish oil. That stuff is good for hair and skin along with your heart, but those pills make you fish burp like you've got a hatchery in your gut."

"You were going in," David said.

"I told her I was going in to find you, and she tried talking to me, but she had a real craggy voice. I'm pretty sure she told me to be careful around the house and said she was learning a language. Real strange."

As Samson spoke, David saw Ted take an interest in the box of ashes on the coffee table. "I said, 'What's that, Fran?' and she tried again, but her voice was totally gone. She made a talking motion with her fingers."

Ted tried to read the label on the package by turning his head to the side and then his body, leaning forward, arching slightly, trying to go unnoticed. He was across the room from the box and squinted toward the small print. David watched him.

"It was kind of strange, but I figured the girl was getting

some secondary education," Samson said. "Spanish or whatever. I said that was good, and she smiled real wide and nodded. Then she went around back."

Ted stood up then, one arm stretched toward the box of ashes. Before he could get closer, David took the box up and moved it next to the window. "Clutter," David said.

Ted watched the box as David moved it but didn't follow him over. "I could have sworn you two owned a dog," he said.

"She learning Spanish?" Samson asked. "That's good for the service trades. We're trying to get the boys into it in school." He drained his beer, becoming aware that Ted was standing. "Got to be hitting the dusty trail," Samson said.

They each warmly shook David's hand, and he walked them to the door feeling that they had all learned something.

"David," Samson said. "It's been so good to see you."

"It's been good to sit down with you," said Ted.

"About that letter you sent us," Samson said.

"About that." David tapped the doorknob with his shirt-sleeve and then unlocked it. "I'm sorry about that. I didn't know you two still talked. I've been a little off lately. I thought that if I wrote the same letter and only one of you came, I wouldn't have to worry if the content of the letter was at fault. I hope you understand."

Ted waved him off. "Not that, David. That's all fine."

"We did have a question about one element of the content," said Samson.

"There is a mention of five hundred dollars," Ted added.

"The money," David said. The men regarded one another.

Samson clasped his hand on David's shoulder. "Thing is, the old gal and I could really use a little help. The kids all need

braces. Orthodontists, you know? I'm frankly not pulling it together at work. We've been losing clients with the tax breaks
drying up, and now college is coming. My wife's looking for
another job, but in the meantime—"

"The mortgage is killing me," Ted said. "I am literally dying every time I stick a stamp because of how much money I
put in envelopes every month. I feel my heart rate speed up.
Kids aren't cheap. Millie wants violin lessons. And would you
believe it, her spine's all twisted up like a pretzel. Needs one of
them things for her back. They say it's a genetic thing, but nobody on my side has it."

"You guys need the money," David said.

Nobody liked to hear it out loud. Samson cleared his throat
and grasped the door's handle, inspiring a subtle sweat in David.

"We don't need it. We're doing fine. Only thing is, you
mentioned money," Samson said. "We were just following up.
We know you've been out of work, but we figured you had
some saved up, living here and all. We were just following up."

"I brought the letter with me," Ted said, going for his back
pocket.

David took out his wallet and extracted his spare checks.
"Don't worry about it," he said. "I know you both have obliga-
tions." He lifted his knee to the doorframe and wrote two
checks for five hundred dollars each. "Please, think of it as my
gift to your children."

The men accepted their checks without comment. Samson
folded his into thirds and placed it in his breast pocket, and
Ted slipped his unfolded into his wallet. They each shook
hands with David in turn. Samson sighed and looked as if he
was about to speak, but he closed his mouth.

The men left, holding the railing on their way down the stairs. David came out onto the second porch stair and watched them walk to their car. "We should do this again," he called after them. Ted turned back and waved, tucked his wallet into his back pocket, and then waved again, opening the car door. Samson kept his back to the porch but raised his gloved hand to the window when he was in the car. David waved back and saw it all as a good sign.

39

AFTER HIS FRIENDS WERE GONE, David noticed that the woman from the salon was sitting on his porch. She had been sitting around the corner of the house, so Samson and Ted likely wouldn't have seen her upon their departure, but David saw the corner of her salon apron, the cuff of her blue jeans. A thermos and a bag of pears rested by the chair. He walked down the porch steps and approached her from the lawn, eye level with her sensible shoes. "I showed myself a seat," she said. Her lips were broad and pursed. He remembered how he had seen an ear within them, which seemed like a strange thought in the daylight but not fully outside the stone-walled boundaries of possibility.

"Aileen."

She stirred the tea in the thermos with a tiny silver spoon, which she slipped into her apron pocket. She reached into her lap and held up a pear. The fruit's colors seemed too bright against her hand, but he accepted it and placed it on the porch. "I saw you walking in the park earlier," she said. "You seemed happy. It looked like you wanted company."

The rocking chair she was sitting in had dug small grooves into the porch over the years, little imprints in the wood that made the chair rock on a track. It made it so the seated individual could rock back and forth within the track, but if he or she tried to shift the chair in another direction—to face the top of the street instead of the corner—the chair would find its groove again and slide back into place. "Who were those men?" she asked.

"Friends."

"You should eat that pear."

"Thank you. I just drank a lot of water, though."

"They are delicious this time of year."

"Too much water, really."

She looked toward the driveway. "Frances's car is gone," she said, running her fingers along the upper hem of her salon apron at the point where it tied around her neck. "I brought you some pears," she said. "You have a lovely home."

He watched the mechanism of Aileen's leg from his position beside the porch. "City took the car."

"I've been thinking about Frances," Aileen said. She rocked with one leg crossed over the other. The toe of her sneaker touched the ground. As she flexed and pointed her toe, David saw the calf muscle engage. "I keep thinking about Frances. We used to drink a cup of coffee before the customers showed up in the morning. She brought different types of nondairy creamers for us to try."

David remembered his own morning routine at the dental office. "I miss her too."

"Because I have a lactose issue." She touched one of the pears in its bag with the tip of her sneaker. "It's unlike Frances to go out the way she did."

"I guess endings don't always follow the story," David said. "Some people don't spend a day of their lives in a hospital until those last two weeks. Everything is different at the end in a way that hastens its coming."

"Still, it was unlike her to go outside in the middle of winter, wearing what she wore." Aileen pointed and flexed and sipped her tea. "She wasn't wearing any shoes, right? She was out there barefoot, in the middle of January, snow on the ground."

"How did you find that out?"

She waved her hand, scattering steam. "It's all online. I was remembering the time I went out to get the paper in my slippers and they soaked through. I gave myself pneumonia. Right then. I could feel the virus enter my body through my foot. It was the worst feeling of my life, what I remember of it. Every day, if I was aware of my surroundings, I actively wanted to die. Frances brought me movies she rented from the library and told me to keep them as long as I wanted. She sat with me. And something got her out there in the snow without slippers on?" She held her face upward. "I'm messing up my face," she said.

"She didn't have pneumonia."

"I know. Athlete's foot, cedar allergy, hypothermia, wounds, but no pneumonia." She saw his look. "Police files, online."

"Why would the police release that information?"

"You'd have to ask them, David. Probably to get the national media involved. I figure we haven't had a satellite truck in town since the last Harvest Fest. Now there's a spectacle to get people interested, show the men and women of our police force frowning and shaking their heads. They have this video of your house all lit up at night. It looks beautiful. They keep showing it on a loop."

"They're filming my house at night?"

"It really does look beautiful, you should check it out. A real winter scene, cozy. Right at the end it shows you walking past one of the front windows." She pointed. "That one, I think."

David wrapped one hand around the porch rail's column. He determined that with the correct angle of approach, he could reach through the columns, grab Aileen firmly by the sneaker, and pull her out of the chair in one motion. "This is an invasion of privacy," he said. "They're trying to smoke me out."

"That would suggest you were hiding something, wouldn't it?"

"I'm not hiding anything."

"Well then, they're only curious."

"It doesn't make sense that what they're doing would change based on what I'm doing."

"Smoke is in the eye of the beholder." Aileen laughed. "I just came up with that. Would you believe?"

David looked at the bag of pears. They seemed different from the ones he had just bought, somehow smoother and more perfect, as if they had been created in a laboratory. He was worried that she would want to watch him eat one. He had his suspicions about Aileen.

"You have such a beautiful home," Aileen said. "How much did you pay for it?"

"My parents dealt with some of the mortgage," David said. "We were taking care of my father."

"What a treat to live in a place like this."

"We would rather have had our own house. It was good to help out when we could."

"Well, I'm sure you were a big help," Aileen said, standing. "I believe it's time for my nap. I'll leave you to your afternoon in your beautiful home."

"Have a safe trip," David said, watching the woman walk away. She left the bag of pears on the porch. He considered leaving them there but feared she might return and see that he had. He picked up the bag and took it through the kitchen and out the back door. One by one, he threw the pears overhand into the woods.

40

DAVID HAD CARED for every tooth of the ones he loved.
When he visited his mother, he brought his dental tools in a
leather bag and performed a cursory exam with her lying down
on a couch in the common area. He could wheedle and plead
and get his father in for cleanings every eighteen to twenty
months, but Franny kept her yearly appointment. Her teeth
were the healthiest he had seen, including gum-model sets in
brochures he displayed in the office. They looked and felt
stronger than the resin models on the shelf. He would observe
her X-rays after she left, experiencing the keen sense of pride
one might feel with a child. He considered framing them in
the office, but he knew that other patients would feel envy toward
the perfect teeth and might even blame David's expert care
for the sugar and neglect that brought them in to begin with.

His father's teeth were a model of such neglect. A lifetime
of dental abandon had started early, when David's grandmother
claimed that toothpaste was an unnecessary and vulgar expense. No matter how advanced the dental water jets and waxed
flosses and prescription pastes David pushed upon the man,

his father's teeth aged poorly with him. David used to watch his father breathing through his mouth in the chair by the window, cultivating scores of bacteria in the deepening crevices, parts per million untold, the invaders shoring up in preparation to go to work that night when the man would lay his obviously unbrushed mouth on the pillow, smacking his lips, saliva rushing forth and infusing the mouth with the moist warmth of an incubator, the perfect environment for a healthy population of ruin. "The dental profession is a farce of control," he said when his son tried to show him the problems.

David had started to remove his father's teeth at the beginning of his career, from when he took his first trained peek into his father's mouth. That first tooth, a maxillary third, rotten through the root, a bruise on the X-ray. The hygienist leaned back in her chair and looked at David wordlessly, ticking the suction in the direction of the spot on the light box after David had already seen it, of course, the blemish an embarrassment on his young career, the father of a dental professional experiencing such advanced molar ruin. He cleared his appointments for the rest of the afternoon and performed the procedure immediately.

His father provided little input beyond what David suspected, which was that he didn't want a metal rod in the jawbone, an exact copy replacing the rotten tooth. The man waved it off even when David told him it would last a lifetime. He reminded his son how old he was, cited the cost of titanium. "Decay comes for free," he said. "Any further installation is vanity." There would be no titanium, but David insisted on making a bridge for his father, placing the Novocain with a practiced hand, filing down each tooth on either side, making the impressions. He installed a flipper to take the place of the missing tooth while the bridge was being made. His hygienist handed off the tools and watched with her hands folded over her stomach. David's gloved hand pulled back a dry tuck of skin at the corner of his father's lip. His father's eyes were closed for the duration. David saw the other problems in the mouth, years of accumulated calculus building like cedar shingles at the base of each tooth, imperfections despite regular cleanings, which could lead to a life of discomfort, agony even, the kind that could silence a man in his chair.

Through his father, David learned that the final years of a human's dental development were a stanching of unstoppable decomposition. The entire practice of dentistry had more of a natural cycle to it when a life span was closer to fifty years. When medical science evolved to carry the lives of individuals past their eightieth birthdays, dentists were the ones tasked with maintaining the appearance of healthy teeth against the mounting years. They became architects in those last thirty years and artists in the last ten, describing the curve of a tooth and its natural pigment with molds and materials. They were cosmetic artists, sculptors, possessing an accomplished level of imagination and skill. David took pride in his ability to see the perfection in every flawed mouth.

41

IT SEEMED REASONABLE to assume that Franny was somewhere in the world. If it was possible for her to be contained within a canister of ash on the table, it seemed equally possible that she was taking a walk in the neighborhood, or that she was out for a drive, or perhaps standing in line at the grocery store with faceless individuals who might fail to recognize the miracle that stood beside them holding a gallon of milk.

David was sure that if Franny was outside, she would be pleased to learn that he had been out looking for her. In the event that she arrived while he was out looking, he left a note at home, asking her to stay. He wrote that if she was there, she shouldn't leave—that he was there, that if she was there, he would find her. He folded the note and placed it in an envelope on her pillow, in their bed.

He found a pair of quarters in the tray where he had once deposited his keys and wallet daily. There was a small handful of them in a coffee cup on top of the refrigerator. In the junk drawer, he found the roll they used when the dryer was broken and they had to go to the laundromat. He thought about that warm room.

He collected enough money and walked to the bus stop. There, he found a person lying on a pile of broken-down cardboard. The person was wrapped in a mound of damp clothes. The stop occupied its own terminal space of sidewalk, jutting up against a guardrail and the stretch of road, meaning nobody would ever walk by unless they were waiting for the bus, and then they wouldn't walk past the bench to the corner, where the person had arranged or found the cardboard pile, which looked like it might not travel easily. It was a lonely corner of sidewalk. The person had spread plastic bags like a flotilla under the cardboard, keeping it dry. David could not determine if the person was a man or a woman. The person didn't move when David sat nearby on the bench. A storm was coming and the air was quiet.

He looked at the person. He put his gloved hand over his face and rubbed his lips with the fabric. "Have you seen my wife?" he asked through the glove.

A wintry mix fell from the sky. Wet turds of snow landed at his feet. The person's hair held a fuzzy corona of ice. There was no evidence to suggest that the person had a home.

It felt like a miracle to spend real time outside in the snow. There had been snowfall for months, but David had watched most of it from inside. As the season had progressed, the first flakes stuck and vanished into uniformity, then car tires made ribbon tracks down the road, then the general cover connected the world in a formless mass. He thought of the formless mass that had been created by the shape of his wife under a tarp, emergency workers chatting around her like guests at a party.

After she had been there, it seemed easy enough that she could be anywhere.

"This atmosphere is a miracle," he said to the tires of the arriving bus. It was not totally clear that the person was alive. "The bus is here," he said to the person, whose hands were wrapped in plastic bags. "The bus is here," he said, waiting for the door to open and then reaching for the stair's rail, depositing five quarters, and waving off the transfer.

The laundromat was crowded with people doing their last loads before the storm hit. They sat with their backs to the window. Washers rattled within their prescribed spaces and dryers spun, radiating heat into the room in an inefficient way that was still comforting to the people, who removed scarves and heavy coats and put spare quarters into the pinball machine in the corner or bought small, bright packages of laundry detergent or dryer sheets from a vending machine, or orange sodas from another vending machine, or peanuts and chocolate from a bulk vending machine by the door. The room was dominated by machines that operated by quarters, and this pleased David, who felt like a wealthy man with his pocket full of the land's standard currency. He bought a packet of fabric softener and a handful of peanuts that, upon closer inspection, were cashews.

He examined the face of each person in the small room, but none of them resembled the woman he had seen the first night. The laundromat wasn't the kind of place where a person put down roots.

Sitting there, David came to the slow realization that he had not brought any clothes of his own to wash. It seemed likely that soon enough, the attendant might notice he wasn't using any machines, was simply sitting in a plastic chair watching the kids play pinball, and the attendant might call the police. The thought made David nervous in a way that was immediately actionable. He stood and walked to the other side of the room, where a folding table was ringed by men and women arranging clean clothes into baskets.

David approached one woman, who noticed him and was already shaking her head at the look on his face.

"I'd love to help you fold your clothes," he said.

"No," she said. "No, honey."

He looked at the woman next to the first woman, her friend it seemed, because they looked at each other and then the friend spoke. "I'm not going to let a crazy man fold my clothes," she said. The women laughed, and David laughed too. "No offense," she said.

"You don't have to be crazy to fold clothes," he said. "But it helps."

"I don't care how crazy you are, as long as you're working for me," said a third woman, so small beside the folding table that it seemed as if she would be more comfortable underneath. "Come here," she said, and David saw that it was the woman from the first night, Shelly, and she was wearing earth tones again, and he had not seen her from across the room because she was much smaller than he remembered and had been hidden by the machines.

"How are you?" David asked.

Shelly pushed a pile of warm shirts over to him and he picked one up. "Sick and tired," she said, glancing at him. "You know, you could probably stand to do a load or two while you're here. I have some spare shirts if you need."

"I'm fine."

She shrugged and returned to folding. "Some days I'm mostly sick, and then it hits me how tired I am. Opposite sides of the same rolling coin."

The shirt he picked up was long-sleeved. He held the collar and flipped the sleeves back. "I feel more tired lately," he said. "People keep coming to my house."

"Not like that," she said. David widened his grip on the shoulders, but she shook her head. "Here," she said, digging into a bag at her feet and hauling out a clipboard nearly the size of her torso. She took the shirt and flattened it on the table, positioned the board in the center, and folded the sleeves inward. She tucked the shirtsleeves back, flipped the board over, and slid it out in a smooth motion, leaving a perfectly folded shirt.

"I'll try again," David said, reaching for the folded shirt.

She snapped it off the table and laid it in her rolling basket. "You'll find no utility in going backward," she said. "Move forward." She prodded the pile.

He took another shirt, positioned the clipboard, made a few false starts with the sleeves, but placed them, flipped the shirt over, and removed the board.

The woman clapped once. "There you go," she said. "Soon you'll be doing it without the board. Soon you won't even need your eyes. There's a goal."

The two friends on the other side of the table snickered but stopped abruptly when the small woman pointed at them. "You won't always your eyes," the woman said. "You lose everything you love in the order in which you love it." David finished another shirt and the woman patted his arm. "You're so kind to help," she said. "So kind, without expecting anything in return."

He felt kind, though her words made him wonder what he could expect in return. It was possible this woman knew something about Franny, had seen or spoken with her on one of Franny's trips to the laundromat. He pictured his wife with a load of towels from the salon, a bag stuffed full of curtains requiring the delicate cycle. He imagined her measuring cupfuls of detergent and bleach into the industrial-size washer, loading quarters into the machine, and settling down in one of the yellow plastic chairs with a magazine advertising a pill you could take to make your eyelashes grow faster.

"The expression on your face," Shelly said. "I could eat it."

David held up his hand to the offer. They folded shirts while he thought about Franny propping her feet on a rolling cart or wiping spilled detergent from a machine with a towel and dropping that towel into the wash with the rest. Franny's eyes shone when she saw him folding from across the room. "You moron," Franny said, smiling, beatific. She was holding an incisor in an oversize antique gold tooth extractor.

"Listen, I don't see you for months, and this is some—"

She raised one finger to her lips and he was quiet. The extractor seemed heavy, and she leveraged her elbow into her side for support. David could see that her arm was spotted with wounds, like cherries dropped over a field of snow. The marks clustered around her wrist and pinpricked all the way up her arm and into her dress, which draped her body in ivory. His mouth dried suddenly, as if he had swabbed it.

"What happened to you?" he asked.

She shrugged. Her saint's smile skewed and she lifted both arms, hefting the tooth and its extractor skyward, exaggerating the shrug, a move that showed David the red marks on her other arm as well, a constellation blooming red, spreading and darkening as the blood dotted in individual pools and then broke through their membranes and streamed down her arms, veining together and dripping down her elbows, her arms lifted, the extractor in her fist raised to the ceiling in a pose that David realized now was a bleeding diorama placed for him.

He clenched his teeth but could not make a connection from molar to molar. His inability to grind the teeth to powder inspired a closed-mouth scream, pushing the air from his body in the scream until his vision spangled and his balance shifted, at which point he became aware of pressure around his body and realized that the women in the laundromat had surrounded him. The two friends were holding him by the arms, restraining him while Shelly was trying to push her gloved hand into his clenched mouth, leaning into it and pushing as hard as she could against the barrier of his jaw. Others stood and cheered, blocking the exit.

Shelly whacked him on the jaw with the palm of her hand as if he was a dog. The indignity of it made him slacken his face. She laughed, but the women were still gripping him by both arms, moving him toward the door. One of them said, "God damn, but you are an idiot," and the other said, "Get it right out of here."

The other people in the laundromat moved out of their way. He bent his arms at the elbow to grasp the bar on the glass door so the three of them wouldn't crash into it. The friends increased their velocity at the threshold and threw him out, his feet leaving the ground with the force of their outward motion. He landed unevenly and tumbled down, skinning his hand on the parking sign he had grasped for stability.

"I'm sorry," he said. A pinkish hue welled into his hand, then a line of blood.

One of them waved her hand at him with a *go on* motion and headed back inside while the other held the door open. "You scared that old lady," she said. "Shame on you."

"Tell her I'm sorry."

Now the other one waved her hand. "You're not watching where you are," she said, closing the door behind her. He assumed she was speaking figuratively until a tall Weimaraner on a leash stepped gingerly on his stomach with a front paw and then a back paw as he progressed.

The dog's owner approached on the other end of the slack leash. David couldn't see the man's face from his position on the ground. "You were in his path," the owner said from above. Dog and owner approached the end of the sidewalk, looked each way, and crossed the street.

42

THE POLICE STATION was centered in the main town square and surrounded by a constant stop-and-go flow of traffic. The building, which was the color of old oatmeal in a jar, had once been the town's first bank. Inside, dusty marble floors matched the walls and baseboards stained with neglect. The building was a hundred years old, and few improvements had been made to the electrical map over the course of its life. Schoolchildren on station tours blinked when they entered the dark rotunda from outside. They bumped into one another, necks craned back toward the domed ceiling.

David took the stairs up to the third floor. He liked the sound his feet made on the marble steps and thought about installing similar stone in the primed, ready stairwell of his own home. Franny would find the stairs extravagant. She might not even recognize the place when she returned to it. She might leave the house, keep walking down the street, and lose herself in the woods.

The stone and the sound it made gave the room a feeling of permanence, as was the purpose of its design. He imagined how similar the old police station would remain after the end times came to pass, for example. He had been taught as a child that the end times could come to pass at any moment. A strong structure would stand even a spiritual test. The horsemen might knock down some file cabinets and vaporize all the nonbelievers, but the marble flooring would survive.

The third floor was a hallway of doors leading off the rotunda. Behind the doors, individuals sat behind desks, determining when to investigate private citizens. David saw a pair of uniformed officers and followed them into the detective unit. At the front desk, a boy was using the side of his hand to organize a pile of staples on the desk, brushing them off the surface and into one of the watercooler's paper cones. "Do you have an appointment?" the boy asked.

"I don't. I'm here to see Detective Chico," said David. "He might be expecting me. My name is David, young man."

"You don't have an appointment?"

"Sorry, is the receptionist here?" David was bad at guessing the ages of children but estimated this one to be between six and fourteen years old.

"You'll have to wait," said the child, dropping the paper cone into the trash and taking up the stapler again, ejecting staples individually onto the desk. He pointed at an empty seat on a bench, next to a woman hunched over a clipboard.

"It'll just take a second," David said.

The child switched the stapler to his nondominant hand and jabbed toward the bench with his stronger pointer. "I'll let the detective know you're here," he said.

David sat. The boy frowned and resumed his stapler task, ejecting spent staples one by one until the stapler was empty.

He took a new paper cup from the watercooler and filled it again, bringing his face close to the desk to focus on his task. When the cup was full, the boy dropped it into the trash, slid off his chair, and walked into the back room.

"Your best bet is the awning behind the trash compactor in the alley on Fifth Street," the woman said. She was wearing a purple tracksuit. The map on her notepad was dotted with stars and skulls. "Sometimes you can score in the hallway in front of the ATM in the city center, but that's rare because there's all this light going right into your face, right into your eyes." She smelled like a bucket of peaches in an advanced state of decomposition. "You'd think there on the corner of Fifth where those kids hang out by the grocery would be a good spot, but cops are always watching there. They got cameras, and inside each camera is at least two eyes. I saw a camera with three eyes once, but the third eye was busted and kept rolling around at the top of the lens. I was trying to fix it but the two other eyes called for help. You ever ask a stranger to look at your tongue?"

The boy was back at the desk. He was taking a pair of safety scissors to a piece of construction paper. "That's enough," he said.

"I'm worried," she said, tearing off a sliver of paper on the edge of her notebook and packing it into the side of her mouth.

"I'll look at your tongue later," the boy said.

"Are your parents around?" David asked him.

"Depends on how you define 'around,' and how you define 'parents,'" the woman said. She turned in her seat, shifting from hip to hip, chewing. "Depends how you define 'missing,' depends how you define 'dead,'" she said.

The boy began searching for something in the recesses of his desk. "Quite enough," he said.

The woman was scratching her face with her pencil; then she threw the pencil into her lap and clawed at herself with her fingernails. "I'll get you started," she said. "Christ, scratching is the resurrection."

Chico emerged from the back room. "David," he said. "What a pleasant surprise. My executive secretary said you were here, but I didn't believe it until now."

The boy slumped. "Why didn't you believe me?"

The detective gestured for David to follow. "Only a joke," he said to the child. "We'll talk about it later."

Chico's office was dark and dominated by newspapers and pieces of books and maps and photocopied stacks of paper, all of which encroached on his keyboard and side cabinets. The paper mounted an offense against his coffee, jutting over it, spare pages drooping over the steaming mug. The room smelled of ink and paper clips. Chico picked a stack off of one of the chairs and balanced it on a smaller stack on the edge of his desk. "Doing some catch-up this morning," he said. "I'm glad you came by. What can I do for you?"

"I want to know what you know about my wife." David nudged folders on the floor until he had enough space for his feet.

"The autopsy came back," Chico said, still standing, flipping open a file. "She was found with multiple lacerations on her arms and legs. Massive laceration on the right-side femoral artery, which killed her." He tapped the top of his right thigh. "Something caused by a dull blade, sad to say. No drugs in her system. Some vegetable matter in her stomach, also objects like thin cloth or paper, about the size of a berry." He tapped his pencil on his desk. "A small berry."

"Cloth or paper?"

The detective shrugged and flipped the page. "Matter like what gets eaten by stomach acid for five to seven hours. We couldn't get anything out of it. The rest is stuff you already knew. She was barefoot, hypothermic. She would have lost her toes had she survived the event." He looked up. "We can slow down if this is bothering you."

"The woman in the lobby was eating paper."

"I doubt the two events are related. It's important to think about potential meaning." Chico leaned back in his leather chair and scanned a bookshelf that had been bolted to the wall between them above the desk. He stood and pulled out a thick book, holding the shelf with the other hand for leverage, hefting it down. "Here we go." He flashed the cover of the book at David, who saw only the gold-trimmed stars and half-moons before Chico turned it back. The book itself was thicker than the old-fashioned dictionary he remembered open on a podium in the library at college.

The detective hefted the book from one hand to the other and cleared a space on the desk. "The interpretation of dreams," he said, thumping the book down. "It always has some truth." He examined the tabs on the side of the book and opened it, flipping pages and running one finger down the columns of text. "Here we are. Paper. The oracles say that dreaming of blank paper means grief. That could mean worrying about grief, anticipating grief, progressing through grief. Dreaming of paper with words on it means great joy concerning a love affair."

"That's it? Either grief or an affair?"

"That's what it says."

"Those two options seem to be kind of in opposition."

Chico shrugged.

"Does all printed paper suggest one or the other?"

"You're thinking of that letter you found in the sugar. 'I will strip the bark from a tree and make you new clothes,' right? Did you find any more of those?"

"You have it memorized."

"It was memorable."

"That's the only one I found."

The detective leaned back in his chair without breaking eye contact. He slipped his finger under the right-hand page in the dream book and turned it. The scent of old ink rose up and mixed with the paper clips. He was watching David. Chico's closed mouth moved slightly with the mandibular workings behind his lips, which were thin and colorless in the low light. They parted into a smile, front teeth tucked. "I want us to be friends, David."

"I trust my wife."

"You should trust your wife. Respect her memory."

"I saw that woman Marie."

"Right," he said, closing the dream book. He picked a business card from a stack and handed it across the table. "She wants to see you. She has some ideas. She can be incredibly helpful with memory." David looked at the card:

MARIE WALLS

TRANCE REGRESSION THERAPY

1201 Southland Dr.

(Garage)

"This is my address," David said, standing to leave.

"Indeed it is."

"She's in my garage? Why wasn't this mentioned?"

"It had yet to become pertinent."

When David stepped outside, he felt the cars slowing before they reached the stoplight. Passengers turned their heads toward him, though drivers stared straight ahead. An older man sitting on a park bench in the square adjusted the manual lens of a camera in his lap. A pair of pedestrians viewed him askance, dragging bloodhounds. A woman dipped her head into a reclining stroller, adjusting a device. Joggers spoke discreetly into their wrists. He was being watched.

43

DAVID HAD CLOSED UP THE GARAGE behind the house years earlier, when wasps took over the high-beamed ceilings. Franny always parked in the driveway anyway, and he kept all the gardening tools in the yard shed. They shared the opinion that killing the small wasps and destroying their paper-thin structures wasn't worth the body count or the overall effort. When he opened the wooden side door, he felt as if he had placed himself ten years back in his own personal history.

Marie was sitting behind a desk in the center of the garage. There were papers and framed certificates stacked on the countertops and shelves where he had once kept the power tools and laundry detergent. Wasps flicked David's ears and settled on his shoulders. Marie stood with her hand extended. "So glad to finally see you," she said. "I have a vision problem that presents itself unless I'm under fluorescence." She pointed at the industrial tubes overhead. "It's perfect," she said. She was wearing a professional-looking blouse and blazer over a pair of pressed slacks. The wasps crawled across her neck and swarmed her hair.

"You're in my garage."

"Are you sure it's yours?"

"I'll have to call the police."

The wasps settled like rings on her fingers. She waved a hand, scattering them. "Detective Chico knows all about it. He comes to see me."

"Who said you could be here?"

"I embarrassed myself not half an hour ago," she said. "I saw you walking a charcoal Weimaraner on a black leash."

"That wasn't me."

"Noble beasts, Weimaraners."

"I don't own a dog."

"I called out to you and you didn't respond. Of course, others are never quite who we think they are. That was particularly clear to me not half an hour ago. I was taking in the air outside the office at the time. I'm much happier to be inside."

"My garage."

"I'm here for you today. Sit down, please. Tell me what's going on."

He remained standing. "For your information, you're trespassing." A wasp crawled into David's ear and he stood very still, waiting for it to come out. He watched her without speaking.

"I hope you're not angry," she said. "I certainly hope you're not angry. This is all entirely legitimate in the eyes of the law. I have the paperwork around here somewhere. Your wife rented this place to me a few years back, and I made it clear that I would never make my presence known. Your wife thought that would be easier on the family. You'll find all of this in the contract. My condolences, by the way. I have that contract here." She opened a file and withdrew a stack of pages. They looked like the receipts from Franny's automotive file.

165

The wasp tickled the tiny hairs lining David's outer ear canal. He could feel the individual legs as they muffled along the delicate cavity. He clenched his teeth.

Marie flipped the pages over. "Really, this is about your wife. It would be more along the lines of respecting her wishes by allowing you to find me. I was so sad to hear about your wife. She seemed like a mysterious woman. Of course you know. She was the kind of woman I'd like to know better, the kind who doesn't lay her whole life in front of you like she expects you to pick it up and figure it out. You know? Some people like to build a lifetime of decision patterns. Your wife was not like that." Marie covered her mouth against a sudden swarm. She waited for them to pass. "I can see why she decided on you," she said once the wasps lost interest. "You're kind of a blank slate yourself, aren't you? It takes the right kind of woman to get a man like you. To understand. I imagine you didn't find too many dates when you were younger. No offense."

The wasp crawled out of his ear, and David immediately plugged the ear canal with his finger, preventing reentry. "Mighty hell," he said, scooping at his ear with his fingernail. "You've taken up office in my garage. The police know about it. My wife arranged it. That's where my world is right now, right at this moment." He shuffled his feet backward so as not to step on any portion of wasp. "I came in here for plywood and a can of paint. That's what things are looking like currently," he said, half turning to check the side door. He saw a can of spray paint beside the door and picked it up. "What are you doing here?" he asked, attempting to wedge the can first into his jacket pocket and then into the back pocket of his jeans. He unzipped his jacket halfway and tucked the can inside. "Chico mentioned you had been thinking."

"Oh dear, I'm always thinking." She gestured for him to sit. "That's the thing we forget about ourselves. I wanted to get into your head the day that Franny had her accident. What were you doing that morning? Where was your mind traveling?"

David shook the spray paint can as he thought. He had spent a fair piece of time considering the moment itself and the moments that followed, but not the time prior. He tried to clear the paths of his memory. He saw the images from a distance, as if he was standing outside the window in the snow. "I can't remember," he said.

"It's in there somewhere. Think about the objects you were looking at, the way you were dressed. The paramedics said they found you in your robe and slippers. A flannel pajama set. Think about the food you ate that morning. The coroner's office said they found berries in her. Were there berries in the house? Picture yourself opening the refrigerator and looking inside."

He did as he was told but could see only a more recent picture, of a heel of bread and a carton of orange juice, two bottles of beer. The food featured thriving mold spores. "I don't know," he said. "Orange juice." He heard a wasp and cupped his hand over his left ear.

"Typical distressed transference," Marie said. "ISV-2034. Your brain has wrapped a comfortable piece of fabric around where long-term memories are stored. I can help you remember. I'd like to try a process with you called hypnotic induction."

"You want to put me in a trance?"

"I think it can allow us to go back to the place before the event. It can help you feel more connected with your wife. Have you ever experienced the power of induction? We can learn so much from so little."

The lid on the paint can popped off when he shook it, and he bent down with some effort to pick it up. "I don't have time at the moment. Perhaps another day."

She shrugged. "I'll throw in a few *gratis* sessions of bad-habit elimination or pain alleviation. We could get you over that thing with the doors."

"Another time. Thank you for your kind offer. Have you seen the plywood?"

"No rush. During the season, I get some research done. I think the word 'you' has been linked with more devastating sentences than any other in the English language. But it's possible that 'love' is worse. I'm feeling it out. It requires some reading." She tapped a stack of anthologies and novels.

David saw a phone book in the stack. "Fine, that's fine," he said. "I've been unknowingly funding research. Do patients come in here? I've never seen anyone."

"I'm still getting the word out. It takes a while to build a common base. Meanwhile, I expect my findings to be published by the end of the year. That should help draw people in, I think."

"Plywood?"

She pointed toward a stack leaned up against a far wall. "Mind the wasps," she said.

The wood looked sodden from across the room, but the boards were dry and fused together on closer inspection. He pried the top one from the stack. He coughed and hefted the dusty board up, spreading his arms, leaning back against the surprising weight.

"I'll be going now," he said, maneuvering sideways, arms spread against the wood grain, the board pressed against his body. It smelled like turpentine and rot. "Good luck with your research. Thank you for being in my garage. I don't know what to tell you."

"I'll be here," she said. The door closed between them. David saw a piece of paper wedged under the door. He leaned the plywood panel against the building and dislodged the page. It had been wrapped around wasp corpses, which fell to the ground, separated from and followed by their fluttering wings. The paper read:

```
IN THAT HALF SECOND WHEN YOU REACHED FOR THE
DOOR, I CAME UP BESIDE YOU, DRILLED A HOLE IN
YOUR HEEL, AND ATTACHED A TUBE THROUGH WHICH
I AM CURRENTLY COLLECTING YOUR BONE MARROW.
IT IS GOING INTO A BAG. I AM GOING TO SELL IT.
```

David twisted around to examine his heel. He looked back toward the house and into the ash trees behind the yard. He balled up the note and kept it in his fist as he walked toward the house.

The house was quiet. David added the balled-up note to the collection in the silverware drawer. He went through the house, touching each piece of exposed metal he could find. He touched doorknobs, window sashes, picture frames, electronic equipment peripherals, door hinges, wall-plate screws, light fixtures, and vents. He put his palms on the water heater.

He touched faucet handles, smoke detector battery connect points, individual razor blades, numbers on clock faces, towel racks, and zipper pulls. He imagined all the metal in the house melted in a cauldron. The mixed alloys would create a speckled bubble, like a stone he once found on the beach and kept in his jacket pocket for years, touching it gently with the tips of his fingers, until one day he put on his jacket and reached for the stone and it was gone.

44.

THERE WAS A RACCOON in the entry hall. It startled David because it was roughly the size of a healthy baby and was plundering the glass-walled base of the grandfather clock. David thought for a moment that it was a baby, there in the shadows. It was bigger than a breadbox. Its fur was slick. Its paws fumbled and grasped. The raccoon knew it could get into the grandfather clock. It was not bothered that David was standing very close, though it did stop and turn toward the light when he opened the door again. David wondered idly at the percentage chance that it was rabid. It seemed likely. Everything seemed likely. He closed the door and walked toward the kitchen with his back against the wall, giving the raccoon a wide berth should it try to leap for his face. Once the door was closed, the animal turned again to its scrambling task.

The kitchen was colder than the rest of the house, and David saw that the window over the kitchen table was still empty from where Samson had removed the broken glass and frame. Leaves and dirt were scattered on the table. The raccoon had eaten most of a pear in a bowl before knocking the bowl to the floor, where it split into three ceramic pieces, curved like the cupped palms of hands. David pictured the startled raccoon making a run for the entry hall. Everything made sense. The empty space where the window should have been gave the kitchen the feeling of being outdoors, as if the kitchen had sprung organically from the ground. Woven branches created natural furniture and older trees formed a refrigerator. All of it was cold, the way it was meant to be cold at that time of year in that part of the world. It felt natural. Still, it wasn't safe to have an empty place where a pane of glass had once gone completely unnoticed. The house could fill with raccoons. If Franny returned, she would assume the place had been abandoned.

When David returned to the entryway, he saw that the raccoon had successfully opened the grandfather clock and was rooting around its base. The clock's pendulum brushed against the animal's body and the gold chains draped over it like ornaments on a woman's coat. The clock's glass walls extended almost to the floor, as if the raccoon had put himself on display in a museum.

45

NEXT MESSAGE. From, phone number three three zero, seven two three, eight nine two three. Received, January thirteenth at nine-thirty-two a.m.

Hello, sweet dear. They're letting me call. I'm sorry to bother you. There is an issue with the bill that you must come by to address. I haven't seen your darling face in so long, darling. My life, my angel on earth. My lovely. Do you miss me? I miss you. I remember when you were a younger man. It's good to remember. Where are you? I've been here all along.

Message erased. Next message. From, phone number three three zero, eight four five, three four three three. Received, October fifteenth at eleven-eleven a.m.

Hey. Please wash and prep the vegetables before I get home. We're in a hurry. Sorry. See you.

Saved. There are no more messages. Main menu. Listen, one. Send, two. Personal options, three. Call, eight. Exit, star.

First saved message. From, phone number three three zero, eight four five, three four three three. Received, October fifteenth at eleven-eleven a.m.

Hey. Please wash and prep the vegetables before I get home. We're in a hurry. Sorry. See you.

Saved. There are no more messages. Main menu. Listen, one. Send, two. Personal options, three. Call, eight. Exit, star.

First saved message. From, phone number three three zero, eight four five, three four three three. Received, October fifteenth at eleven-eleven a.m.

Hey. Please wash and prep the vegetables before I get home. We're in a hurry. Sorry. See you.

Saved. There are no more messages. Main menu. Listen, one. Send, two. Personal options, three. Call, eight. Exit, star. To indicate your choice, press the number of the option you wish to select. Whenever you need more information about the options, press zero for help. You can interrupt these instructions at any time by pressing a key to make your selection.

46.

AILEEN did think of the salon as her child. The salon was needy, like her grown children out of state, old enough to know better, calling at all hours, always finding new ways to break down.

After a long day at work, rush hour in the small town was the worst. It was chaos compressed into the smallest space possible. Getting caught in traffic meant sitting through three long lights and a busy train crossing. Aileen sat at the first light with her chin hooked over the steering wheel, squinting forward.

It had been one of the longer days in a line of long days. One of the girls had accidentally sprayed keratin treatment solution into the eyes of one of the salon's best clients, who ran for the shampooing station, hollering and scrubbing at her face, grasping blindly, trying to operate the sink controls. Aileen calmed the woman down and then had to take the afternoon interviewing for a new aesthetician. The candidates gawked and showed too much tooth. She asked one woman what she would do if confronted with the morning's product accident and the woman jutted her chin forward and said she had no clue.

Aileen resisted turning the rearview mirror toward herself. She knew the outside light was highlighting her face in a way that would define the age spots and give her wrinkles a deeper shadow. She could see the furrow deepening between her eyes, even under the carefully applied layers of pro-mineral foundations and powders. Her new year's resolution had been to be brave and give up the syringes of filler, so accessible in a drawer in the treatment room. They were full of toxins, of course, but that never upset her—she hated that furrow in a way that made toxins seem wholly appropriate, ideal even, a chemical weapon for an enemy combatant. It was a war, she reasoned, while convincing herself to take the injection. Afterward, she would observe her smoothed face and feel ashamed, cowed, cowardly, ineffective, rationalizing. In bed at night, she imagined the toxins seeping into her heart.

She was stuck at the longest light in town, longer for rush hour, allowing northbound traffic to escape the city square. A city bus inched along within the line, and Aileen examined its passengers as they advanced one by one. There was a lineup of heads facing away, a young girl slumping, an older man reaching for the bell cord. Behind the man, Aileen saw Frances.

It was such a natural feeling, so clearly Frances, that Aileen's first thought was that Frances didn't ride the bus. Yet there she was, smiling, touching her hair as if she was aware that she was being watched by a friend, a favorable eye, one that had missed her. It took a moment for Aileen to place Frances within the timeline of events. As she did, Aileen's hand lifted to the car's windshield. She pounded on the glass, startling pedestrians in her line of sight as she called out, fist against the windshield, calling toward Frances on the bus, who looked like a photograph now, hand frozen in her hair, obscuring her face, a prop of a woman in a moving vehicle, a mean joke but a good one, Aileen near tears with laughter or near laughter with tears, the two states of emotion so close that they shared a border.

Aileen reached for her door, tugged the handle, found herself locked in, and banged on her driver-side window with an open palm. The bus was moving then, pulling away. She fumbled with the lock until it released, and she tried to step out of her vehicle but was restrained by the seat belt, so many things holding her back. She screamed at the seat belt and the bus, threw the emergency brake and unbuckled, and was finally out of the car, waving her arms at the driver, leaping over the curb into the grass bordering it, trying to get his attention, though he had already progressed through the intersection and was merging into the turn lane and was gone.

Drivers behind Aileen had given up honking and began to maneuver around her car, rolling down their windows to yell at her on the sidewalk. She could hear their noises as they drove away. A man approached her and said some words, but she did not move from the curb. She watched the corner where the bus carrying Frances had vanished, and then she sat down on the sidewalk and twisted her knuckles into the concrete. Her skin curled back and bled like all skin bleeds.

47.

THAT WINTER featured the kind of cold people forget
about during the rest of the year. Franny would haul the wood
and David would make a fire and both of them would promise
themselves that they would always remember the feeling.

David remembered another such winter, when they lost
power and burned old greeting cards in a bowl for light. Franny
had kept the cards in a shoebox but spoke often of throwing
them out to eliminate clutter. There were yearly birthday greet-
ings from her parents, seeming store-bought and inauthentic
despite unique signatures. They burned nicely. Franny found
letters on fine stationery from a great-aunt long gone. The aunt
would conserve postage by fitting a year's worth of news into
one letter, writing on all sides of all accessible space, a postscript
on the back of the envelope. David and Franny read each piece
of correspondence aloud before burning it. The ink made the
flames glow green and blue.

They swore that night that they would better appreciate the
warmer months for the way they forgot their bodies. David remembered that during an illness he swore that he would remem-

ber the swollen and aching feeling in his chest and legs and throat, that he would appreciate the days when he could breathe without coughing or walk without stumbling. Then those months of wellness and heat came again, and he did forget, as they eventually forgot that winter when it was gone.

48

ONE AFTERNOON, years before, all the juice glasses in the cupboard shattered simultaneously. The sound it made was of a single powerful firework followed by a garbage boat advancing slowly through ice. David had been out front, painting their mailbox, and he assumed it was children rolling a large stone or a small car onto the thawing pond at the end of the road. It was one of the early sunny afternoons during that first year David and Franny had the house to themselves.

Franny was the first to see. She had been in the living room, packing books for storage, taking her time to open each and looking for envelopes full of money. She wouldn't put it past David's mother, though the woman had never mentioned such a possibility during her brief meetings with her daughter-in-law and in fact hadn't been in the house in years.

When the glass broke, Franny dropped a book pertaining to the travels of the saints. The force had blown open the kitchen cabinets, and she could see that each level was layered with shards. She took a step into the kitchen and onto a thin layer of glass. It was clear that moving her bare foot would drive the glass farther in, and so she existed on the glass in a way that was simultaneously precarious and painless. She called for David.

The thick tumblers at the base of the cabinet were crumbled into sparkling chunks. Glass dust lined the counters and floor, varying from tooth- to palm-size. The room was silent, as if the shards held a power to absorb sound. Franny opened her mouth and closed it without speaking to David, who was standing in the doorway of the far side of the kitchen. He ran around the side of the house and in through the front door. She was too far away to reach and so he laid his heavy coat on the floor, stepped carefully on it, and guided Franny down to sit. He put his arms around her and dragged her out of the kitchen. Then he brought his old dental examination light up from the basement and spent the evening tweezing glass from his wife's feet, dabbing the cuts with isopropyl alcohol, depositing the glass onto a plant saucer he had found on the front porch. She cried a little at first and then got over it and read to him from his old saints book while he worked on her.

There had been no movement of the earth, no discernible change in pressure. An unknown explosion, and then broken glass. A few wineglasses belonging to Franny's parents came away with hairline fractures, suggesting that the blast must have had a low epicenter.

Franny was convinced that someone had entered the house while David was painting the mailbox. She held his shoulder and told him that there had been an intruder, that the intruder had obviously entered through the front door and walked by Franny in the living room without her knowledge, a theory that made her feel as if the intruder had made actual physical contact with her, held her against a wall. She imagined the intruder was a small but powerful man who wore ski pants. The intruder would have stolen the ski pants from another home or perhaps a store, putting them on under his jeans and walking out, maybe even waving to the cashier, cavalier, his stocky legs insulated with stolen goods. Franny said that it was time to buy a security system. David considered the possibility of wiring the doors in the house and adding an electric current that could be broken and restored on a whim, by a machine. She talked about security cameras and motion detectors while he thought about the impartial entity observing them making love or eating breakfast.

She felt nervous about intruders even when they learned that the destruction had been caused by the water heater in the basement exploding, the percussive force directly below the kitchen having the same effect of balancing their glassware on a timpani and striking the instrument with a mallet. While David pulled glass from her feet, she spoke of intruders and security, and the exploded heater quietly flooded the basement ankle-deep with hot water. The man who came to replace the heater suggested that they hire a cleaning crew before more papers were ruined and walls damaged, but the expense was too great and David removed some of the water with a bucket before allowing the rest to more or less drain out the door in the den, where the foundation dipped low enough to allow some liquid exodus. The basement had too many problems to fix. The flood was another in a long line.

Meanwhile, Franny laid out plans, drawing diagrams of the house. It became clear that she had thought about it for a long while prior to the glass incident. David explained that any system was out of the budget and therefore out of the question, but for many months afterward she kept the plans on the bathroom counter. She had one image, of the full house layout, which she was particularly proud of. She had placed gold stars at the most likely points of entry, places where they could point cameras. She had the layout framed and hung it above the dresser in their bedroom.

49

THE PLYWOOD did not affix easily onto the space where the
kitchen window had once been. The nails couldn't puncture
the siding. Upon closer inspection, David found a ribbon of
steel wrapped around the window opening. Anchoring lag bolts
were required, and the cordless drill. David found the items in
the basement, which he needed a flashlight to explore, as the
bulbs were all burned out or broken. He enjoyed a brief fantasy
of walling up the basement entry with bricks, entombing the
mess inside, but the water heater was down there, plus his father's glass jelly jars full of miscellaneous screws and nails and
lag bolts, which he brought to the surface and used to secure
the plywood. Once it was up, he wrote I AM STILL HERE with
the black spray paint, in letters visible from the street, for the
benefit of anyone who might make the mistake to think otherwise. It felt good to cover the place where people might either
observe or enter his home's interior. He wondered if he had
enough plywood to cover each of the windows.

50.

SHELLY FOLDED the last of the clean clothes and placed the two stacks next to each other, the jeans and shirts delegated to separate sub-stacks, folded socks nestled like baby mice around their perimeter. She was the only one in the laundromat again, though a few humming machines suggested that people would come and go.

Her nephew had stopped by earlier with a new load of clothes that had been released from their duties as evidence. It seemed unfair to incinerate them, unfair to the clothes and their former owners, and Shelly requested that each load be brought to her. The shorts and slacks were blameless in her hands. She could rehabilitate them.

A faded burgundy polo shirt extended an inch above one of the folded sub-stacks, and she examined it, frowning, removing it from the stack and pulling it over her head. It made a tight fit over the pair of long-sleeved shirts she was wearing, plus the T-shirts underneath, one of which advertised a theme park she had seen once while walking a long way. She smoothed the collar and felt where the fabric had been torn at the seam.

After she put the polo on, the sub-stacks were perfect. Shelly took out a pocket level and balanced it on top. The bubble hesitated at the center, then settled. She descended from the footstool and walked around the folding table, examining it from all angles. "The line is so clean," she said. Anyone would be pleased to see her achievement. She pulled a chair to the table and stood on it, taking in the aerial view, then plucked the level from the stack, placed it in her pocket, and smoothed the dimple it had made on the top shirt. It seemed as if the shirt had been created for the sole purpose of finding its way there, to the table, to become perfectly folded atop another shirt. It looked like a photograph of a stack of folded clothes, but Shelly knew she had created it from ordinary objects and an idea in her head, and the pleasure of that fact added to the moment.

She knew that only the passing of time would evolve her thoughts on the scene. Crossing the room, she leaned against the far wall and watched her perfect pile. Another woman with a laundry basket paused in front of it and nodded once. Shelly was filled with pride. But time passed, and sure enough, the feeling of perfection began to diminish. It seemed as if the hemline on a folded skirt was slightly askew, peeking out above the rest like a taller man in a lineup. She walked closer and saw the pills of cotton clinging to a sweatshirt. She nudged a pair of socks into order, but the whole thing still felt wrong. In one motion she gathered up the two stacks of clean clothes, turned to the nearest washing machine, and dumped them within. She dug into her pocket for quarters and reached for the soap.

51

COLD MORNINGS grew colder, and the plywood made a poor heat barrier over the kitchen window. It shuddered against the wind and grew damp at the edges. The heater would have worked itself to death, solely for the purpose of sinking warm air into the wooden window. Ants moved in branched lines up the walls toward the second floor. David stopped turning the heater on and went to bed wearing a wool cap.

One particularly cold morning, he got up while it was still dark and put on his ski jacket. He got back into bed, under Franny's coat, feeling bundled, as if he was between a pair of sleeping bags, as if he was camping in his empty bedroom, feeling warm and confined.

The next morning, he brewed a pot of coffee and brought a cup of it to the garage. Marie was writing in a notebook at her desk and looked up to smile at him. It was as warm as a greenhouse inside the garage. David noticed the space heaters mounted on the walls, strung from the ceiling with electrical wire. Power strips lined the garage like rattraps. A massive ceramic-coil heater dominated Marie's desk. The wasps clustered around David's face in greeting.

"Good morning," she said.

He set the mug down on her desk. "Who's paying the electrical bill in this place?" he asked, covering his mouth with his hand as one of the insects came to investigate the source of moving air.

"Coffee. That's sweet of you." She tapped a silver thermos by her elbow. "I have tea already, but thanks anyway." She had a glossy magazine open next to her notebook. There was a column full of tally marks on the notebook. In the magazine, a woman's mouth held a diamond between her teeth. David considered the potential for irreversible damage to the woman's enamel.

"You wouldn't have a wasp problem this time of the year if you didn't have heaters everywhere."

"They keep me company. It's important to have a harmonious work environment. With the heat on, they get more done during the winter than I do."

"How's the research going?"

She shrugged. "'Love' pulled ahead," she said. "I'm recounting. Too early to tell."

A wasp plunged its stinger into the thick wall of David's boot. He bent and pinched it out, crushing it in the process. He flicked its corpse aside. "Have you been leaving threats around my house?"

"You found more after the one in the sugar?"

"They're spreading."

"Well, it's not me. But thank you for asking instead of accusing. I could see on your face that you were intending to accuse."

"You understand how I might suspect it."

"People jump so quickly to the conclusions they wish to make. You finally realized I've been conducting business on a piece of your property. But you're a reasonable man. You understand that things are never precisely as they seem. It's a trouble with people. We get one idea of an outcome in our heads and we can really run with it into the sunset. Fortunately, you're the kind of man who allows things to happen to him instead of forcing them to happen." She considered for a moment. "'You finally realized,'" she said, writing it down. "Exactly."

"There were two threats at my wife's workplace. I wish I would stop finding them."

"If wishes were fishes," she said.

"One was tucked within her personal effects."

"That would certainly lead you to another conclusion." She flipped through pages in her notebook until she found a loose page. "This was behind one of the wasp's nests. I found it this morning when I was sweeping the floor."

She offered it to him, and he took it. The page felt brittle, as if exposed to water and years.

```
CURL UP ON MY LAP. LET ME BRUSH YOUR HAIR
WITH MY FINGERS. I AM SINGING YOU A LULLABY.
I AM TESTING FOR STRUCTURAL WEAKNESS IN YOUR
SKULL.
```

"I don't like that at all," David said.

"It's a dark one."

"And you're not writing these?"

"Are you joking? My mother died of a brain injury. There is no way I'd use it as a symbol." She sipped her tea. "How ugly."

"Who is doing this?"

"Probably it's whoever you least suspect. Or most suspect. I forget how that goes."

"I need to understand what is going on in my home."

She flipped back the pages of her notebook and began to read aloud. "'Your wife made some decisions during her life, decisions to which you weren't privy. That's normal in any relationship. The moment one fully realizes this truth can lead to a difficult transition. You move awkwardly from ignorance to knowledge like a baby falling down a set of stairs inside a bucket,'" She lifted her eyes. "Pardon the expression."

A wasp landed on David's neck and took a circuitous route around his hairline, considering potential nesting points.

"Surely your wife was not writing threats," Marie said. "That doesn't really seem like her, does it?"

"I don't know what seems like her."

"Don't speak, think, or act out of frustration, David. That makes a fool of us all."

He thought about it. Two wasps sparred on the lip of his coffee mug. "I don't know what seems like her," he said.

"You should tell the detective of this new finding."

"I'll tell him when it's time," David said, "and if you want to remain in business in my garage, you'll allow me the time I need."

Marie pressed her lips into a line and regarded David for so long that he thought she had been paralyzed by a stinging wasp. "Fair," she said finally. "You'll figure it out soon."

"My childhood friends say they saw her."

"When?"

"A few months ago. She told one of them that she was learning a language."

"Your friends must have been mistaken." She poured another thermos cupful of tea.

"That's what I told them."

"What was once your wife is currently located in a box on your coffee table."

"Well, that's a tough way to put it."

"Indeed it is." Marie cradled her thermos cup as if it was a precious jewel. A wasp hovered and landed on the frame of her glasses. She didn't blink. The wasp lost interest and flew away.

"Do those things ever sting you?"

She put down the cup and held up her right hand toward David. Her palm was studded with welted stings, swollen red and oozing fluid. "You need someone around," she said. "The human soul longs for comfort in times of grief."

"Are you licensed to practice? Do you have any kind of training?"

"You don't have to be hurtful."

"I'm sorry," David said, "but I don't know why I just apologized."

"Probably some kind of latent boyhood issue," she said. "An anal obsession, maybe. LSV-II220. Let's work on it next time." She wrote down the appointment in her notebook before pressing her hands to her face, blocking out the light. He left her there.

52

AT VARIOUS POINTS over the course of dental history around the world, different cultures were convinced that cavities were caused by worms. There were enough worms manifest in the rest of the body that it seemed possible for very small worms to coil inside a tooth or between two teeth, spreading decay and ruin. The Sumerians believed in the worms as early as 5000 B.C., the Muslims determined that the theory was garbage in A.D. 1200, and the French figured it out about five hundred years later, using microscopes. But there were bright sides to the error, and one of the brightest sides was the glut of beautiful worm-related art that came out of all cultures. One French carving featured a molar, done in ivory, the size of a human tooth. This ivory tooth could be opened to reveal a carved dual scene of the worm itself imagined as a demon in Hell, devouring the impious whole—screaming, pathetic individuals thrown into one of Hell's general fires, perhaps in preparation for the tooth worm or as an alternative fate.

In hindsight, the tooth worm might have done its part to contribute to the ruin of David's dental career. He first saw the

French carving in school, and subsequently, whenever he looked into a mouth, he imagined the coiled serpents. He saw them in the deeply troubled molar profiles of his squirming patients at the free clinic, where he completed his training. He saw them in the texts he studied, in back issues of *Dentistry Today*, in the diagrams and charts on the wall of his office. By the end, he saw them in all of his patients. Individuals with previously clean X-rays came in with teeth that hummed, foreign movement under his explorer.

A pair of concerned parents brought in their little one, not quite ten months old, who cried and didn't take his bottle. There was no pediatric dentist in the area, and the child's father was the son of one of David's father's old friends. David's hands shook with a fear of what he might find. The boy's mother sat in the chair and cradled her son, shushing him and kissing his forehead and then making kissing noises and holding the child's head still. Sure enough, the soft nubs of infant teeth pulsed with the worm. David didn't even need to prod at the new teeth to know they were deeply flawed. A young life spoiled. The child wept and pulled his head away from David's gloved fingers. The young mother started to cry even before David said he would have to administer a local anesthetic and drill the four teeth. She cried out then, when he said it, and her husband came running in from the waiting room and asked to know what was the problem, what had made his young wife weep—he was quite young as well; David realized he was dealing with three young people—the young man heading toward David in a way that suggested he might lift David from his chair and throw him against the wall, on which was mounted an expensive light box that nevertheless still had a problem with the circuitry that caused a flickering and would certainly be destroyed if David was thrown against it, and so David raised both hands, the dental explorer shivering in his left, his right extending toward the young husband, who demanded again what the hell was the problem anyway. David kept his hand extended for a tense moment, and then the man reached out, confused, and shook David's hand. David placed the dental explorer on its sanitized tray. The receptionist leaned in from the other room but David shooed her off. He explained to the young couple the ways in which an infant could develop tooth trouble, perhaps by using the bottle as a pacifier or being allowed to sleep with it. The mother started nodding, though tears were now streaming liberally down her cheeks, the woman weeping in guilty silence, aware as she was of her own complicity in letting the child fall asleep with his bottle, which he loved so much and was sometimes the only way to get him to sleep. After a series of long days for all of them, her discovery had been such a welcome piece of good news. The child would sleep with a bottle! It had to be near empty, just a hint of milk warm against his lips. She had worried about making this decision but remembered the nurses at the hospital and their comforting chorus of "it's your baby" while she cradled the foreign thing, the baby, which was hers.

When the call came in that David's license would be revoked owing to reports of suspected and proven gross malpractice, he wasn't surprised. He remembered the fallen look of the woman's face as he pushed the needle into her infant's jaw, and he knew that this would not be the last he heard from her, that his close attention, his kindness and care, would be repaid with betrayal.

Of course he would fight the charges for years, dwindling his financial resources. It was a matter of personal pride in his work. When he returned from court each time, his wife and his father listened to his stories while looking into middle distance, because they did not understand that it was a matter of personal pride.

He lost the appeals. Nothing more could be said.

53

THE MORNING featured a chill that might try to convince
you to stay down if you happened to slip and fall. The weather
might question your actions as you stretched out on the frozen
path, pointing out that as long as you continued to rest with
your back on the ground, you could see the sky.

The bus stop was empty except for a man reading a map.
The man stood next to the bench, though he was alone and the
benches were wiped clean. He paged through the map a few
inches from his face. He wore the same ivory and blue ski
jacket as David, the same reading glasses with the same band
of electrical tape circling the center bar. The same speckled
gray hair tufted loose over his ears.

"We wear the same glasses," David said. The man had
David's face shape and the same eye color. He was wearing the
same style of clothing, a buttoned brown shirt over brown
jeans and the awful jacket, which featured a rip in the same
portion of sleeve where David had torn his own on a turnstile.
They each wore dark-laced sneakers, but only the strange man
was wearing socks. They looked comfortable and woolen. The

man folded the map, and David handed him one of the two pieces of toast he had brought from the house wrapped in a napkin. The man accepted the toast and examined it before taking a bite.

"I'm sure there's a reasonable explanation," David said.

"You live around here?" the man asked.

"Right up the hill."

"I've been looking to buy, thought I'd have a peek around out here. Nice neighborhood." The man ate toast in the same way David did, first chewing the upper arch of crust, tonguing the butter, and holding the mass in his cheek while talking. The man held the mouthful in his left cheek while David typically favored his right, but it was otherwise a precise duplication.

"It's quiet," David said. "The neighborhood kids are in school right now or else you'd see more folks outside. Even though it's pretty cold. People are friendly here."

The man held the toast up. "Thanks." He took another bite. Crumbs shattered off and flecked his shirtfront. "Aren't you going to ask me who I'm working for?"

"Who are you working for?"

"Nobody."

"Why did you want me to ask you who you're working for?"

"I'm wandering around your neighborhood, I give some idiot excuse about looking for a house to buy. We look exactly the same, down to a level of detail that could not possibly be coincidental. The question seems apparent."

David saw that the man also kept frayed ends on his shoestrings. "But you're not working for anybody," David said.

The man shrugged. "I should ask you who you're working for."

David took a bite of toast. The man took a bite of toast. They chewed and regarded each other. David could see the man packing the bread into his left cheek with his tongue.

"Who are you working for?" asked the man.

"This is ridiculous," David said. "This is not some kind of spy game. I'm taking the bus to see my mother in a home for women, where she has lived now for many years."

"My mother doesn't live at a home for women. Close," the other man said, advancing a step. "You might call it that. But that's not where she lives."

The man had the same deep wrinkle between the eyes, the same mark of a mole at his left temple, matching David's right. The man was a mirror image. He continued to advance.

"I'm not working for anybody," David said. "I am unemployed."

The man stopped advancing. "I have no way to believe you."

"I have no way to believe you, either."

"This is not some kind of spy game," the man said.

A woman bumped into David, and he realized that the bus had arrived. The driver was leaning forward in his seat, watching the two men.

David moved to get on the bus, but the other man stood still. "I'm on the next one," the man said. "I am on the next instance of this bus."

"I think it would be for the best if we avoided seeing each other," the man said to David.

"Any day you want this to happen," said the driver.

"But you know where I live," said David. "You're a visitor here."

"I know the general area. I don't know exactly where you

live. Are you worried about your safety? I don't think you need to be worried."

"Come on, twinsies," said the driver.

David stepped onto the bus and leaned his head back. "Neither of us should be worried," he said. He dropped his quarters into the coin slot. Outside, the man finished the piece of toast and shook out the napkin. He folded it once and placed it in his front pocket. David thought he saw words written on the napkin, but the bus door closed between them before he could get a better look.

54

EVERYONE working at the home for women seemed too young to be there, employed or otherwise. A clean-faced young woman at the reception desk handed David a clipboard and asked him who he was there to see. David pointed toward the meeting area beyond the wire mesh window, where he could see his mother sitting in her wheelchair by herself. The young woman began to speak of a billing dispute. David found a credit card in his wallet and told the young woman to keep it. The young woman seemed satisfied. In return, she gave David a nametag. He affixed it to his shirt, and the woman buzzed him in.

His mother had a blanket over her lap and faced a table on which playing cards were spread facedown. One by one she turned over each card, touched it, and placed it back on the table. At another table, a group of ladies even older than David's mother drank instant coffee and compared miniature figurines from their collections. Workers were taking down tinsel and cardboard cutouts of trees and placing them in boxes by the front door.

"Mom." He settled into a chair across from his mother.

She tipped her face up at the sound, smiling in recognition, holding the king of spades. The crevices of her spotted face sunk farther under the light. She was wearing her heavy-framed glasses, as she had for years, despite the blindness.

"Hello, my love. What brings you to paradise?"

"I wanted to check up on you."

"I'm fairly busy today. I should have some time open up in the afternoon."

"I brought you something." David produced an Apollonia medal from his pocket and slid it across the table. She placed the king of spades lightly down and reached toward the sound. Her hands found the medal and she touched it with care. "Now isn't that sweet," she said. Drawing her hands back, she picked another card from the table, running her fingers along the edges. "Two hearts," she said.

David ducked his head to see the card's face. "How did you know?"

"It's an old trick, my darling. An old trick on an old deck. There are slight discrepancies in each card. One edge of the two hearts waves a bit. Someone may have dipped it in their tea." She picked up another card and touched the edges, then the face and the back. "Seven clubs," she said, turning it twice for David to confirm. "There's a mark on one side, in the center. A hairline scratch. That's the interesting thing about seven clubs. Seven diamonds has a scratch on the far side, closer to the edge."

"How do you know all this?"

"One of the nurses helped. The girls said I could play bridge with them, and I'm going to give them one hell of a surprise."

"Here I was thinking you had some use for those glasses."

She touched them. "The weight is a comfort."

"I'm glad you're doing well, Mom. A lot has been happening."

"I'm doing so well." She palmed another card. "Slight bow, ace spades."

He looked. "Ace of hearts."

"Darn, ace hearts. Ancillary bow." She tugged on a blanket wedged under her in the chair and pulled a corner of it over the blanket on her lap. "The girls have been teasing me," she said.

A group of ladies on the other side of the room were passing around a small crystal horse. Each woman in turn lifted the piece up and shifted it slowly to catch the light. She murmured her approval and sent the trinket on to the next woman.

"A lot has happened in the past few weeks," David said.

His mother placed the card on the table and felt with four fingers the way it bent back. "How is your dear wife?" she asked. "Is she keeping up with the housework? You sound a bit tousled."

"She's fine." David watched her stroke the playing card. "She's doing fine. I actually was thinking about the house."

"My sweet child."

"I keep finding things I wouldn't expect to find."

His mother shook her head so slowly that David followed the direction of her eyes toward the corner of the room, where a worker was sweeping tinsel from a countertop into a paper bag. "That darn house gave us trouble from the first day we bought it," his mother said. "You know that foundation problem didn't turn up in the inspection? That was a major issue.

We could have sued the city, but I was too busy taking care of you and your dad. And then your poor sister," she said.

"You did a good job."

"I was among the busiest women on the planet. Did you know? They wanted to give me an award for how busy I always was. They invited me to a reception, but would you believe I was too busy to go? Those were different times. I would have had to buy your father a suit and one of those bow ties. Cuff links too. I already had one nice dress. Nice enough, you know."

"You did everything you could do," David said.

"The doctor begged me to take medicine for my sleep. I didn't want to, because I got so much work done at night, but he practically got down on his knees. Of course, I was obedient. It was that time for women." His mother touched another card but didn't pick it up. She turned her head toward the ladies. "They're playing hide-and-go-seek," she said. "Hide until someone dies. Everybody. Don't you think?" One of the ladies heard her and glared.

"Mom."

"Would you believe I was too busy to go to my own ceremony?" She coughed, gripping the legs of the chair. "For the award. Your father would have required a different type of shirt than the type of shirt he owned. I don't require you to believe it, but I suggest you do."

"I believe it."

"Of course you do, my sweet." She placed her hand flat on the table in David's direction and then picked it up and put it on the cards again. "You were always a good boy, even when you were a little difficult."

One of the other women across the room cleared her throat. David touched the arm of his mother's wheelchair to turn her away from them. The foreign movement caused his mother to murmur, both hands held still in her lap. David leaned in. "The interesting thing about one hundred forty-three," she said, "is that it is the lowest quasi-Carmichael integer you will find in base eight."

The blanket had fallen off his mother's lap and David adjusted it, tucking it at her side.

"The interesting thing about seventy-eight," she said, "is that it is the smallest integer you can write in three different ways as the sum of four squares."

David crouched closer to his mother's face. "I know it seems like a bad time to talk, Mom. I wanted to ask you a few questions about the house. It's important."

She paused and lifted her face. David saw the full constellation of broken capillaries. Her glasses caught a piece of fluorescent light and illuminated a square on her cheek. "The interesting thing about one hundred seven," she said, leisurely drawing a hand up to scratch the side of her face, "is that it happens to be the exponent of a Mersenne prime."

"I'll come back later," David said.

His mother's murmuring voice was barely audible. "The interesting thing about seventy-six—" she said as he stood to go.

He peeled his nametag off and crumpled it over the trashed tinsel.

55

IT ALL DEPENDS on the conditions of the wash. On the twentieth wash in hot water with a strong detergent, a delicate shirt is known to split at the seams. However, mix the same shirt in with cool water and the proper cycle, and the shirt can last five times as long. A miracle of modern fabric technology. And to think, women used to blanch their hands with lye.

Shelly picked the pills from a sweatshirt she had washed five times that morning. She didn't look at the back of the shirt, which had three slashes across the upper part that almost looked like they could have come from aggressive moths. The fabric felt slick, as if there had been too much detergent building up. She made a note to run it through a cold-water wash without chemicals, to clear everything out.

The regular crowd worked silently in the laundromat. A young woman corralled kids out of rolling baskets and toward the pinball machine. Two college kids, a boy and a girl, paged through thick anatomy texts while waiting on their individual spin cycles. Shelly had a sock full of quarters tied around the belt on her waist. The sock was so heavy it caused her to lean.

She untied the sock and fished four quarters out with the tips of her fingers.

The college boy was watching her feed clothes back into the machine. "You already did that," he said. "Ma'am?"

Reluctantly, she looked at him.

"Those are all messed up. Those clothes," he said.

She saw that he had a terrible haircut. "Do you ever get the feeling that something isn't quite right?" Shelly asked.

The boy shrugged and looked back at his book.

"I'm serious," Shelly said, waiting until she had his attention again. "Do you ever get the feeling?"

"Those pants have a big hole in them," he said, pointing.

"Have you never, not ever stood in the center of a room and looked at the people looking at one another and gotten the feeling that something was badly wrong?"

"You should throw those socks out. My grandmom says red wine stays."

"Listen," Shelly said. "Think about the way a group of people can look at one another. Think about just a pair of people, how they can sit in a room and stare. These are not strangers to each other. They have spent nights sharing their secrets. They see each other and think of those complexities, yet there is nothing that can truly draw them together. It's a primary flaw of human distance. And what causes it? It's not from a lack of desire for closeness. For most of us, closeness is a major life goal. No, there's some additional factor causing this separation. Could it be what we eat for breakfast in the morning? Could it be the mechanism of the human eye? Who's to say that it's not the condition of cleanliness in our clothing? My hypothesis is built on the concept that there is an element of comfort inherent in our dress that contributes to our closeness."

The college boy thought about it. Not everyone did. Shelly wanted to give him some credit for that. She dug into her sock for a quarter and placed it in the boy's hand. "Thank you for thinking about it," she said.

The boy smiled and said nothing, which made her want to give him credit again, but she stopped herself and turned to finish loading the rest of the wash instead. As she moved shirts and jeans into the wash bin, she thought about the young man as he might appear later that day, standing in a room and doubting the motives of his closest friends. The thought filled her with such joy that her heart welled up, and two small tears dropped into the wash at such a perfect moment that she felt certain it was the end of the world's connected problems.

56

THE HOUSE shifted in the dark. Drifts of dust gathered in the corners of the windows and thickened with the moisture in the air into a damp sludge. On one west-facing window ledge David found a dry layer of dead flies. He wrapped them up in a few squares of toilet paper and threw them into the trash, their bodies crushed together between his fingers, forming a new kind of body.

He had to dig the television out of the basement. He knew it was under the workbench, which itself was pinned under stacks of documents that had once, in theory, been essential. He burrowed into the top stratum of utility bills and found a layer of patient X-rays he'd brought home after cleaning out his office at work, when he rented a van and had everything moved out within six hours, the girls standing in a silent line watching him, snapping their sugar-free gum. He had loaded the last of the supplies and applauded the girls before loading himself into the van's cab. He clapped for them wildly, with genuine feeling. One of the hygienists curtsied, but the rest stared, arms crossed. They had just lost their jobs, after all.

It was not legal to keep patient records at his private residence, particularly considering the manner in which he left the practice, but the X-rays had been too meaningful to leave to the industrial shredder. He thought of them as art objects, blue-tinged, individually flawed. He had known all the teeth in his collection, thousands of teeth, enough to fill a bathtub or pave a road. He thought of an ivory paved road leading to some foreign city. Franny's cooking magazines made a glossy layer under them. Under that, delicate pages from years prior, Franny's mother's old recipes, their ink blanked with time. They tore like tissue paper when he moved them. The television was underneath.

David brought the television set upstairs and placed it on the coffee table next to the package of cremains. He plugged it in and adjusted the bent antenna until he got a picture. A game show was on, and he watched a family clutching one another and calling something out toward a screen. The volume dial on the set was missing, and he couldn't figure out the rules of the game. He watched the family hold one another and weep. The evening news came on, and he watched spectators walking around a plane crash. The scene changed to one of a horse being brushed by a woman with long hair. The horse was beautiful and the woman was all right. He watched the weather, where more snow seemed to be suggested by a tired-looking man wearing a red blazer. The picture changed again, this time to a dark screen, and David leaned forward to adjust the contrast and then realized that it was his house, filmed at night. The caption read "Police Question Husband." He used his fingernails to turn the knob where the volume dial had once been, but the speaker had been crushed by the pressure of the elements that had been stored above it, and all that emerged was a low buzzing sound. He watched as, exactly as Aileen had described, the camera pulled in to reveal his own shadowy figure moving behind the curtain of one of the illuminated front windows.

"I'll be," David said. He watched himself standing, watching the road. He imagined the newscasters speculating on what he might be thinking at that moment by the window, which had stretched to include all moments. He would need to do something to hinder the intrusion of the world outside his home. He thought of Franny's security plans above the dresser, then of the plywood in the garage. He thought of Marie in the garage.

The old television had markings on the sides, where David as an eight-year-old had carved into it with a penknife. David's father found the vandalism, smacked his son's bottom with a newspaper, took the knife, and hid it. This was right after his mother left for a week and right before she left for good. The marks were glyphs dug into the side, pictographs transcribed from top to bottom, which David had made while his father was in the basement and David was in the living room, watching cartoons designed to fully occupy his brain.

David touched the incised grooves with the tips of his fingers and then the palm of his hand. He tipped the television to its other side to see if he could read more of the old markings but instead saw a deep inscription that must have been made with a professional engraving tool:

I COULD DEVOUR YOU.

The threat was carved vertically, letters stacked over one another like a totem display. Each carved letter featured individual flaws yet seemed perfectly uniform in relation to the others, as if the engraver had made light pencil marks and later wiped them clean with a rag.

It was immediately important to David that he leave the room. In the kitchen he ate a pear. It occurred to him that, though he had eaten hundreds of pears in the past, if not thousands, this pear was different from every single one he had ever eaten, wholly unique, and, in fact, as he ate it, he was opening parts of the pear that had never been experienced by anyone, human or animal. When his maxillary incisors pierced the skin, which first protected the fruit as it had against rain and sun and then yielded to the invasion, he was oxygenating particles that had never even been open to oxygen. The wet fruit and seeds had existed in darkness for their entire lives until he tore them out with his teeth.

57

LONG AFTER the other detectives had come and gone and the cleaning crew stopped in to empty the trash bins, Chico remained in his office, paging through the dream interpretation book. Marie had asked for a few statements of meaning for their next session. He looked up "tree," "forest," and "clothing." In his notebook he wrote "transitional phase," "searching for understanding of self," "wasting energy," and "perception of public self." He could smell the pages of the old dream book and the rot in the walls around him. It was dark outside. He drew a line through "wasting energy."

Staying late that day was more of a moral requirement than an above-and-beyond kind of display. Chico had spent most of the day standing at the window and wondering which finger he could do without if he was forced to make that decision. He didn't like the look of his left thumb, but it seemed the pinkie finger on his nondominant left hand had the lowest use profile of any. He examined the finger's nail. It was a fine digit overall, but he could do without it if necessary.

It seemed unfortunately possible that David was capable of

doing harm to his wife. Chico had failed to discern a motive or means, but the possibility was there, which made it an option worth considering. Women seemed to make David particularly nervous. Though he did not seem to display a violent tendency, it was worth noting that a nervous individual was capable of performing surprising acts. And then there was the hereditary potential toward premeditated violence, stemming from the actions of David's mother, which Chico maintained had not been an act of insanity, despite what a team of well-paid lawyers flew in to suggest. They convinced a jury of the woman's peers of the insanity defense, which Chico had never suspected would transpire, given the woman's total lack of insanity, in his opinion. On breaks from the trial he saw her doing her taxes, producing a small calculator from the pocket of her professional slacks.

In the reception area, the child was cleaning the floor with a miniature push sweeper. The device whirred forward and back. The child was singing a song about friendship, which he had heard on the radio.

Chico considered what he had learned about the woman Frances. She was tall and quiet, stubborn with coworkers, and distant with her husband. She kept secrets. It seemed equally possible that she was capable of doing harm to herself. A woman with the right personal motivation could walk into the cold and die. Stranger things had happened before and since.

He walked into the reception area, where the child was emptying the reservoir of the sweeper into a garbage can. "I'll walk you to the laundromat," Chico said.

"I believe I'll stay here tonight," the boy said.

"Come on, someone will see you. CPS is down the hall."

"I have a change of clothes. I was looking forward to this all day." The child moved his chair to reveal the sleeping bag under the desk. "You can't force me to go with you. I have the paperwork around here somewhere."

"Your aunt will be worried."

"She knows all about it. She praises me for my dedication to my career."

"You should be going home and playing video games and eating popcorn, or whatever kids do."

"My aunt makes the point that next to a laundry room, there's no safer place than a police station." The child snapped the reservoir shut on the sweeping device and tucked it behind the desk. "Good night, Detective," he said.

Chico remembered a story about children who slept in a museum, and the bitter jealousy he had once felt toward those children. He shook his head at the child but put on his coat. "There's sugar cereal in the break room," he said.

The child was already tucking himself in. "I know where the sugar cereal is," he said from under the desk.

58

MARIE BARELY FLINCHED when she felt a wasp sting the palm of her hand. "Bastard," she said, waving it away.

It was unfair to bees that stinging anything caused them to remove a portion of their own abdomen. Marie couldn't imagine being so angry that she would be willing to give up part of herself like that. The wasps had it easy. They could punish without consequence.

The wasp stings swelled less each time. The initial pain was the same, but the aftereffects were more manageable. She speculated that her natural allergy to the venom was slowly decreasing. She examined her palm.

She rubbed her temples with her unstung fingertips as she read from a set of texts. She always got to the garage before sunrise, finding that the act of setting aside proper hours helped her focus her mind and streamline her efforts. That morning, she had watched David carrying plywood boards into the yard. He leaned them against individual windows and stepped back, seeming to estimate their scale against the frames. Marie raised her hand to him, and he returned the gesture in silence. She felt calm watching him, which surely meant that he was also feeling calm, even as he spent the rest of the morning driving nails into the frame of his home.

She saw David's action as the good sign that he still needed to feel some security in his world. When the loss of privacy was still felt, the self was still known to exist. She thought that was a good thing to think and had gotten as far as writing "privacy" in her notebook, plus three of its synonyms, when another wasp stung her. "Sweet bastard," she said.

59

DAVID NAILED THE LAST BOARD in place over the last window. His home was ready for any storm. On the four boards across the front of the house he sprayed I AM STILL HERE, as he had on the rear window, in text large enough to be seen from the street. Those who saw the boarded-up house thought of a number of things.

A neighbor walked her dog in front of the house. She could see a man descending a stepladder in a robe and slippers, holding nails in his mouth, steadying himself on the ladder. It was the house she had seen on television, which meant this was the man police wanted to question, though she couldn't remember why.

The mailman parked his truck outside the house hours later and loaded up his saddlebag to walk the street. He saw the house and was reminded of a trip he had taken to the beach. He was just a child then and with his family. They had planned the trip for months, but when the winds and rain picked up, they had to leave early. He had watched the boys from the ice cream shop layering boards over the windows.

A child walking home from the bus stop saw the boarded windows and stopped to stare. She had seen plenty of windows in her time but never any covered with long sheets of wood like the kind her father kept in the garage. This was a strange house, she knew, having once seen a woman in its backyard pulling up her robe to step over a fence and getting stuck and dropping the snowballs she was carrying and crying the way the girl never cried anymore, because she was a big girl. The girl thought about how good it felt on an early morning when the first peach-colored lines of the sun said good morning through the curtains and how that meant it was time for milk that her mother mixed a powder into so it turned chocolate-flavored. The girl wondered why anyone would want to miss such an event.

The man who resembled David walked by, holding papers advertising the sale of nearby homes. David had already gone back inside, but the man saw the boarded-up windows and thought about how they might affect property values. The house looked like a dead face to him with the boards, and the man thought of the time he had nearly drowned.

A pair of older ladies in matching tracksuits paused on their speed-walking route to observe the house. They were sisters, and each saw the house and remembered simultaneously when their own childhood home had burned to the ground. Neither could remember how the fire had started—they had been too little, it had been in another city, another state perhaps. They had returned months later with their father and had seen how strange the charred white clapboard looked, boards nailed over the window frames. The new wood had been nailed to old wood, and the distinction was clear to everyone.

The ladies looked at this different boarded-up house in the neighborhood where they had lived together ever since. In silence, they individually considered the span of their lives. One of the ladies thought about the word "still," and the other thought about the word "here."

60

THE DARKENED WINDOWS shifted the home inside further. Even the heavy curtains had let in some light, but the boards allowed total darkness and safety. David thought about how his life would be different if he had boarded up the windows ten years earlier. Perhaps the outside world would have vanished for Franny and himself and they could have lived their days in the confines of the property in his name. He figured that if Franny came back, she would be surprised to see the windows boarded up, but she would eventually understand. The dark outlines of the furniture in the rooms gave the couches and chairs the look of sleeping animals.

The sounds outside were quieter. David could hear a snow sweeper's muted progress along the residential road. It seemed as if he had covered his own ears and eyes with a piece of fabric. The silence of the old grandfather clock was a negative energy. David pushed an ottoman over to cover up the fireplace.

He turned on the kitchen light and pulled the threats out of their drawer, spreading them out on the countertop. He couldn't remember the order in which he found them and switched the papers around trying to figure it out. The threats were on different types of paper. There was the craft store receipt, the fortune cookie scrap, the computer paper, the thin ticker-tape strip, the index card, the pages torn from a notebook. The words were typed in the same style, as if they came from the same machine. He let his eyes unfocus until the words became symbols.

He looked for other clues on the paper. It would be meaningful if he could find out for certain that each threat had been created or printed at the same time. If he could determine the order in which they were intended to be read, he might be able to uncover some code in their language.

David looked carefully at the threats. It was possible that a third party had snuck into the house, created each unique threat, and hid them in each corner while David and Franny were sleeping. It was possible.

61

OBJECTS from the basement had begun to creep into the main house. Before, when the house was full of other people, the mess had been more easily confined. It was as if the others created a gravity and the individual items were an orbiting constellation of junk. In those first years of his son's re-residence, David's father would head down to the basement with a cardboard box and come up with papers and ancient bank records, and he would spend the afternoon inhaling paper dust next to the old shredder, carrying bags of shredded paper to the curb. Every time he went into the basement, he would come up with a new bag of the same general garbage, like a fisherman drawing up a crab pot. "Clean home, old heart," he said.

It had started with the water heater explosion, which caused an inch of bank receipts to plaster the floor. They dried and flaked eventually, their lower layers turning soft and causing the basement to take on the sweet smell of wet newsprint. After they replaced the broken glasses, Franny had remarked that David would need to go down there with a shovel and clean it up, but he didn't, and she did not mention it again. They closed off the basement but scrubbed and dusted and generally maintained the rest of the home's three bedrooms as if they were still all occupied.

After Franny was gone, a layer of dust and skin particles and hair built up over the wood floor. It mixed with the oils in David's feet as well as the dirt from his shoes and his visitors' shoes and gummed together, creating a thin layer of grime that gave the floors a softness. Sticky wafers of grime and hair layered behind doors.

The dust on the floor began to creep up the walls. It fell over itself to make a patina of grime, first on the baseboards, then up the curling lower portions of wallpaper, then broadening to darken the walls nearly to the ceiling. David took a damp washcloth to a portion of one wall, and the single clean swab made the rest look even worse. The moisture from his cloth dripped and accumulated dust, leaving a slick behind it on the way down like a woman's made-up face after a long night of crying. One corner of the wallpaper was peeled back on itself like a filigree, and David took the edge of the paper between his fingers. Behind it, he could see part of what looked like a word. He pulled the wallpaper off the wall and saw another page, yellowed with wallpaper glue, pasted there:

```
I WILL STAPLE MY ADDRESS TO YOUR WINTER
COAT, LITTLE ONE. THEY WILL SEND YOU TO ME
NO MATTER WHAT YOU CLAIM.
```

He hooked his fingernails under the threat and peeled it off, making glue fall, silent as snow, onto the floor. The wallpaper had been there for at least seven years, since he and Franny had put it up together. David moved a chair in an attempt to cover the spot and added the threat to his collection.

Empty broth cans had begun to accumulate around the threats still spread across the countertop. Junk mail lay across the kitchen counters and the table. Bills and notices surrounded Franny's ashes on the coffee table in the sitting room, and the magazines and newspapers were a glossy presence surrounding David every night in bed. He still slept under her coat, but added a layer of dental X-rays under it. It felt as if she was lying lightly on top of him and fish scales filled the divide between his body and hers.

David's body cluttered at the same rate as the house. His hair began to grow long again and curl like a boy's in ringlets above his ears. He washed his clothes at the laundromat, avoiding the machine in the garage. Below the layer of his clean clothes, the crevices of his body began to foster their own microsystem. He began to think of himself as a piece of dense bread.

In the bed, he found himself valuing his inability to move. He might wake and peel a perfume ad or sports page off his face, leaving a wet smudge that he eventually lost interest in cleaning.

He borrowed books from the library about sleep disorders and books about coping with loss. When the words didn't make enough sense, he pulled the pages from the books and lined the mattress with them and kept them under his body at night. He sweat on them, and they offered their insular heat, cells of therapeutic text sinking into his own cells.

He started the bad habit of keeping cartons of food on the bed, until the ants came. Even after he made the effort to clean the cartons away, the ants remained, lost in the pages and sheets, apparently satisfied with the pieces and crumbs they still found. They greeted the corners of his eyes and lips in the morning.

David had always felt uncomfortable in his bed, always shifting his body and stretching his legs. Now that the confinement of paper meant he had nowhere to go, his body became resigned to its diminished accommodation and was held still. He was surprised to find it much easier to sleep. Sometimes he would stay in bed for hours after waking, feeling the proportions of paper around him with the edges of his body. He sensed himself molding the paper into a permanent shape. It was a kind of meditation.

AILEEN was sitting in the rocking chair on the porch. It was unclear how long she had been there, but he remembered registering the sound of wood rocking in the wood groove hours earlier, when he got out of bed. He had thought it was a memory of sound and only realized she was there around lunchtime, when he saw the back of her head through a crack in one of the boarded windows. He tapped the window, and she turned and waved. He beckoned her inside.

"Listen," she said, stomping ice from her boots onto the welcome mat. "Frances put this in my coffee cup in the break room." He shut the door behind her. She dug into her purse and held a handwritten note out to him like it was a piece of identification:

```
I WILL CREATE A SET OF WORK RESPONSIBILITIES
THAT ARE INCONVENIENT AND DEMEANING TO YOU. I
WILL CONVINCE YOUR BOSS TO RUN WITH IT. WE
WILL CALL IT THE BATHROOM SCRUB CHALLENGE.
```

"I think it's about me," she said, flipping the paper back and reviewing the words. "It's embarrassing. Frances and I shared cleaning duties, but sometimes when I was with a client I asked her to touch the mirror up a little. Do you think she was angry with me?"

"I don't think she could write that."

"One of the girls saw her writing it. I found it in my coffee cup months ago and asked around, and one of the girls saw Frances do it. That area is employees only. We don't let anyone else in there. She wrote it."

It was very quiet in the house, and David realized that he had grown accustomed to the rocking chair's constant noise. "May I have it?" he asked.

She held the page closer to her body, against her stomach. "I feel like she would be angry if I showed it to you," she said. "Can you imagine? Maybe it's a bad joke. I would hate it if she wrote this about me. I mean, she wrote it out and everything. One of the girls saw her."

"If she wrote it, I can give it to the police."

"Maybe you could avoid telling them that it might be about me. I'm so embarrassed."

"I'm sure it's not about you."

Aileen turned the paper over, examining each side. She folded it in half and unfolded it. She placed her palm on the words and closed her eyes. It looked as if she was trying to absorb the words into her skin. "I can't keep it. The police should see it. If you really think it will help."

David thought about the threats on the countertop. "I'll show it to the police."

"Thing is"—Aileen looked at the page in her hands—"the thing is that we never called it anything. We would never call it the bathroom scrub challenge. It's so unlike her to be cruel in that way." She folded the page again, rolled it and unrolled it. "Maybe I could keep it. You took everything else of hers."

"You're right when you say the police should see it."

"I saw you had taken everything of hers from the salon. It's fine. You were within your rights. But when I saw, I sat behind the front desk and cried about it. I'm not the kind of woman who cries. This was after closing. I saw everything was gone. Of course, you were well within your rights. The next girl in that room would have put on the apron and put the oils on her fingers without even knowing about them. Really, it's better you took them. But this is all that's left."

He thought of Aileen crying, the LED display of the cash register illuminating her face with a machine-green light.

"I think about everyone who has died where we are." She leaned forward to speak, then leaned back and held her hands over her stomach, clenching the rolled-up threat in her fist. "We make such a fuss when someone dies in a house now, because the proper place to die is in a hospital or a nursing home, or maybe on the street, but never in a house where we spray antibacterial solution on the counter and scrub the floors and vacuum two or three times a week. Two times a week. What a rude thing, to die in a clean house. Better to go to a place where there is a professional level of clean, we think. We've got it figured out. Yet think of the age of the earth and the age of humans on the earth. Think of the number of people in the thousands of years who have died on this very spot. Actually bled out over the ground on which we sit and think about how impolite it is to die in a house. How narrow-minded of us, how selfish." She unrolled the scrolled threat and held it. For a moment it seemed as if she was going to rip it apart.

When she looked at him, he could just barely see the inner ear parting within the sheen of her lips. She handed the page to David, and he felt the warmth from her hand. After she left, David walked into his kitchen. He cleared some of the broth cans from the countertop, where the threats were still laid out like a treasure map. The pages were all different shapes and colors. Some looked as if they had been around for years, while others were crisp and new. The new threat was stained across one edge with coffee.

63

THE SECURITY MAP over the dresser featured points of potential entry and methods of resistance. There was a triple-lock system for the door in the den and a series of traps that could be set around the door if the intruder managed to by-pass the locks. Franny had wanted to board up the workroom door in the basement, because they never went in there and it seemed possible for an intruder to enter the house through the room's small storm windows. The plan included some trenches dug in the backyard. A speculative mark on the side of the page suggested that there was room in the family budget for dogs.

Before he got into bed, David brushed aside a line of ants walking over the pillow. He lay down and felt a piece of the mass more obtrusive than usual against the back of his neck. He reached and pulled out the envelope he had left on Franny's side of the bed days or weeks ago. He took the paper out of the envelope and read:

IF YOU'RE HERE, DON'T LEAVE. I'M HERE IN THE
HOUSE. IF YOU'RE HERE, I WILL FIND YOU.

He held the page to his chest and sensed his body alive under it. He felt a great sadness, which caused him to tear off a sliver of the page and put it in his mouth. He packed the sliver into his right anterior molar and tore off another, a thin strip, which he rolled into a ball and pressed into his left anterior molar. He packed the paper into his teeth again and again until each molar was stuffed full, plus the spaces within the single divots of his premolars and behind the deep divots in his maxillary central incisor. David ran his tongue across the newly smooth teeth. It tasted like he was holding a small book in his mouth. He longed to read his words to Franny again but had eaten them. He went downstairs.

Marie was sitting at the kitchen table. "I wanted to try some coffee," she said. Her hands were stung and swollen to the point where she had to hold the cup by pressing it between the tips of all ten fingers. She brought the trembling mug to her lips.

"Do you need some diphenhydramine?" he asked. It was hard to talk. He clenched his teeth to compact the paper further.

"I'm fine, thank you."

David poured a cup of coffee. The liquid was viscous. "You put too much in," he said. He took a sip and felt the coffee soaking deep into the packed paper.

"I have your best interests in mind. You can't say that much for most therapists. Most everyone else is in it for their perception of a paycheck. I haven't even asked you for any money. Analysis is a passion of mine."

The coffee in his cup was like an oil spill. "We should get you an adrenaline syringe," he said.

"You should come see me again. I'm very helpful, you know. If you release yourself to the potential of help, anyone can be helpful."

Some of the paper had disintegrated into the hot liquid, thickening it further. "This coffee."

"I'm good," Marie said. "I don't even have to ask you a question. Eventually you'll give me everything I want, which is, in turn, everything you need."

David put the mug down and picked up his jacket. "I need to go into town. Could you lock up?"

"Consider it done," she said, jingling a set of keys. David was halfway to the bus stop before he wondered who had given them to her.

64

CHICO WAS IN THE MIDDLE of his after-lunch practice of relocating for twenty minutes to a bench outside the
police station. He had a spiral notebook on his lap, which he
paged through with one hand, reaching into a bag with the other
to throw bread crumbs to the birds.

He was surprised to see David, surprised in that way when
someone is being discussed and they appear, as if it were a
dream. It was a special subvariety of a wider variety of surprise.

"David," he said. "Good morning."

David took a seat on the bench, tilting his head to look into
the paper bag that rested between them. "Bread crumbs?"

"They give bags of them away at the deli." Chico scooped a
handful and scattered it on the lawn. Three brown birds flew
down from a nearby tree and commenced to fight over the
crumbs on the ground. "I learned of your father's passing. Five
years doesn't seem so long ago."

"It was expected."

"Neighbors still remember him fondly."

"He subscribed to magazines about grains."

"Every individual creates a monument to himself in the end."

David shook a half cup of the bread crumbs into his palm and brought it to his mouth. "He was a good man," he said. In speaking, he ejected a tablespoon of crumbs onto his jacket. "My parents were always good people."

"The human ego is an ommatidium, David. Your mother had a lot on her plate. Having children in a difficult time for medical science, the toll that took. Then, of course, the institution, after your sister's untimely passing."

"A home for women."

The detective checked his notes. "That's not what this says."

David leaned sideways to look at the notebook. On the line where Chico pointed, he read *the toll that took. Then, of course, the institution, after your sister's untimely passing.* The next line read *A home for women,* followed by *That's not what this says* and then *If I've learned one thing.* Chico closed the book. "If I've learned one thing as a detective, it's that patience gives your surroundings the chance to give up everything you need to know. Not aggression, not even close attention. Patience." He drummed on his knee with his fingertips. "Are you a patient man, David?"

"You're supposed to be questioning me now. I saw that on the news. Are you questioning me?"

"I have questions, but you surely have questions as well."

"They didn't mention on the evening news that I have questions as well." A bread crumb had attached itself to David's chin, and Chico watched it bob as he spoke. "They seemed less interested about my questions, perhaps because I'm not a member of law enforcement."

"We have some natural concerns. Your wife had no apparent antagonists. No plausible cause stands out. You've been very helpful, but they tend to have questions in the main office."

"Concerns."

"Natural concerns. Sorry, you seem to have a bit of bread on your chin, there."

"I have my own theory."

"Do share."

David scratched his neck. He looked across the street. "She was hiding things from me," he said. "There were financial problems at the salon, and she didn't want to let on. She was losing her grip and creating elements of danger around the house in order to snap herself out of it."

"You seem to be having these thoughts for the first time, for my benefit."

"I have had these thoughts for years."

"And you're saying she did it to herself."

"She got caught in her own trap. It snared her and she lost her mind. I don't think she meant to."

Chico rolled the corner of the bread crumb bag between two fingers. A bird hopped near, regarded the man's fingers on the bag, and hopped away. "That's an interesting theory," Chico said. "Would you mind if I brought some investigators by your house later and we all took a closer look around?"

David stood. "They said on the news that you had a warrant," he said.

"I understand."

"Do you?"

Chico looked at David, shielding his eyes against the winter sun. It looked like he was raising his hand in greeting. David touched the detective's fingers with his own.

AMELIA GRAY

"What's a warrant?" Chico asked.

"It's a matter of personal accountability," David said.

"I understand."

David stooped to brush invisible elements of the park bench from his behind. The single crumb, the largest, remained on his chin.

Chico watched the man's limping walk toward the bus stop.

THE GARAGE was original to the house, which meant it was large enough to hold one carriage and two horses. Over time and industrial revolution and questionable advancement, the space had been modified and neglected in alternating efforts. The roof sagged under years of snow and ice and fallen branches. The partition that had once given each of the horses its own private space now separated the barely functional washing machine from the dryer. Hooks and ropes hung from the ceiling, holding old bicycles and gardening equipment above reach, an impractical storage system that required an A-frame ladder to retrieve anything.

David found Marie lying down in the corner. She had hung a mosquito net from the hooks on the ceiling and spread the net around two wooden shipping pallets she had pushed together on the floor. The gauzy white gave the partition the look of a young girl's room decor. It looked like she had used soap and water to clean the floor and the white-lacquered dryer. The wooden pallets had been stained and varnished. Marie was wearing a blazer and skirt. She looked like a flight attendant, except for the fact

AMELIA GRAY

that she was lying on pallets on the floor. Her hands covered her eyes. David's impulse was to turn and leave, but she removed her hands and looked at him, so he kept walking until he was standing over her face. The wasps walked in individual circles across the mosquito net, looking for their way in.

"I need to know if we have doctor-and-patient confidentiality," David said.

"Technically, you're not my patient."

"Can I become your patient?"

"Also, I am not a doctor. Again, speaking technically."

"I'd like to work some things out."

She rolled onto her side and pushed herself into a sitting position. "I'm glad, David. You are the best judge of your progress in any matter." She held out her hand. He ducked under the mosquito net and tucked it under his heels behind him to keep the wasps out. He shook her hand and she turned to address the wasps. "You have my guarantee of doctor-and-patient confidentiality," she said.

He was aware of the smell of her shampoo. "Do you have the ability to put me in a trance?"

"I can certainly try." She moved to the side of the pallet, careful to spread the mosquito net in a way that kept her from pulling on it when she crouched next to him. "Here, lie down. Close your eyes, hands by your sides."

"Right now? Shouldn't I do something to prepare?"

"The truest result comes from spontaneous action. Careful for splinters."

The wood felt weak and wet under him. He could smell fresh varnish. The pallet stuck to his hair. Eyes closed, he could sense her near him, and then he felt a soft pressure of air on his face, and then he could not sense her near him. He wondered if she had left the garage, but he kept his eyes closed. He tried to slow his breath. If she was still in the room, she was waiting him out. He stayed like that for a while without making a sound. He had a fearful flash that she had gone into his house and was loading his things into a waiting truck. David was certain she had left the room. He resigned himself to the fact that he would die alone in this warm room with his eyes closed. It was comforting to know. He thought calmly of the fact that sometime in the future he would breathe out and would not breathe back in. It became apparent that he could not feel his left foot in its shoe, and he wondered idly in a small portion of his brain if that foot had vanished or had simply died and remained attached to his body. It seemed possible that when he died, the feeling of death would spread through his body like a deep blush, that the blood on its farewell tour of his veins and capillaries would move slowly and with familiarity, like a man leaving a room for the last time, looking at the items he had purchased and arranged, broken or repaired, the man recognizing each before switching off the light.

A portion of his living body heard Marie speak. "Relax," she said. "Imagine you're walking down a long set of stairs. As you walk down the stairs, you realize the air is thickening. Each breath you take in is more productive. Your body fills like a cylinder and presses out through not only your mouth but your ears and skin and eyes."

David thought of his heavy breath like a supply of air emerging from a plastic tube that was curled inside a velvet bag. He thought of the feeling of receiving oxygen from a mask and the calming sensation it brought, partly because of the concentrated gas but partly too because he could hear his muffled lungs expelling their product within the mask, and it reminded him that he was breathing, that the gas was flowing at all times but most importantly at that moment, a constant and essential truth. His lips and lungs and teeth were witnesses to the passage of breath.

He heard Marie's voice as if from a recording. The wasps provided the buzz and burr of static behind her. "Your surroundings are wholly familiar yet strange," she said. He pictured himself on the stairs in his home, descending into the basement.

"The world around you is entirely untraveled, yet you feel no desire to explore it. The mysteries of the world are deeper than your breath, which nourishes your blood and grows your hair and propels your muscles and bones as you guide yourself. Your breath feeds your mind, of which you consciously become less aware, pushing it away, watching it float like a paper boat on a still lake."

David exhaled. Without sight, the light of his mind barely illuminated a shimmer at the base of the stairs. His mind took a step forward and down, toward the lapping water. The stair underneath him was cold. The concrete of the stair and floor held the water in a quiet pool. There was a ceremony in his posture.

"Like a paper boat on a still lake," Marie said. Her voice was very close. "A paper boat, on a still lake. Your mind is a paper boat on a still lake, floating away. Your mind is floating away. You see a still lake, you are a still lake. On the still lake is the still in which you place your mind. Your mind is folded into the folds of a paper boat. The lake is so still that placing your mind in it causes three ripples that extend farther than your eye can follow. The lake beyond is still. You push a paper boat away and watch it float like a float, like a paper boat, a boat on a still lake."

David was aware of Marie's hand on his chest. "Stop," he said, reaching for it. Her hand was not on his chest. He opened his eyes. She was sitting with her hands on her lap. "I'm sorry," he said. "I was just beginning to feel something."

She looked at her watch. "You were down there for a while."

"For how long?"

"I'm not sure. I think I put myself under for a while there. Fifteen minutes?"

"Did I say anything?"

"You kept saying 'Paper boat on a still lake,'" she said. "I thought that was very lovely."

"You were saying that."

"Was I?" She touched her fingers to her temple. "Huh."

David sat up and braced himself on the floor to stand. "Thanks for your help, Marie." A wasp stung his collarbone on the way out.

66

THE INSTITUTION would feed its charges as cheaply as possible. Flat sandwiches housed lonesome rounds of bologna. For the lucky, a bag of chips arrived uncrushed. Carton of milk, carton of juice. Foil crimped on the edges, and peeling it unsealed the professional vacuum. The juice could expand and breathe once before dying, like the oysters men opened at Gulf Coast lunch counters.

At all institutions, the diet-restricted were provided with oversweet gelatin and unbuttered toast. The toast was always perfectly prepared, to the point where one could sense years of toast behind it, an entire lineage of toast emerging from the oven. She thought of her husband while she ate toast.

Food at prisons, hospitals, and similar care facilities has the same nutritional profile. Congressmen fought hard for this nutrition, bringing in experts who would claim that patients needed vitamins and that the brains of inmates required nutrients to make essential decisions in violent situations. The inmate brain on excess sugar could rage like any animal, the government nutritionists would claim, and there it would be, written out on a piece of paper and therefore true. David's mother hadn't touched a noncontraband square of chocolate in years.

She chewed her toast and thought of her husband on his inversion table, arms loose by his head, the skin of his body sinking earthward. She thought of the image of sweet calm on his face at the moment she told him what had happened to their daughter, her own confusion afterward as he reddened and shouted a series of noises that seemed unlike words, pulling his body toward his ankles, so strong suddenly after years of weakness, the chair swinging forward so violently that she barely had time to jump back as he crouched toward his ankles but overswung his weight and tipped hilariously forward, the entire thing askew—she thought he had been so unhappy—the rear supports tipping into the air and sending the upper piece of the machine back to jam into the wall, trapping him inside, his strangled pleading not unlike the sounds their child had made, her husband wedged there in the wall, the image of him crouched in the corner of their home like some wild creature, blood-bearing veins in his body stretched to capacity around his neck and bursting in his eyes.

It had been a violent enough reaction that she refused to speak for days, despite her husband's pleading as to where to send the police. She drove to the motel parking lot and broke into one of the old rooms and took her pitiful few remaining nausea pills and stayed there, horizontal on a mattress, until she heard the sirens and drove home and waited for them to come find her.

As an old woman, David's mother felt ineffective at most things. She remembered her daughter floating in five inches of water, stretched in it, fluid seeping into her little lungs.

67

THREE NEW MESSAGES. One saved message. First new message. From, phone number two three four, seven three two, seven eight four two. Received, February fourth at ten-twenty a.m.

David, this is Aileen at the salon. I want you to know that you know you know what you say you know and I know you know more than you say you know and you know I know you know and—

Message erased. Next new message. From, phone number two three four, seven three two, seven eight four two. Received, February fourth at ten-twenty-two a.m.

David, Aileen. I need you to call me. Please call me. Imagine how much better you'll feel if you do. We'll both feel so much better. We have to get to the bottom of this, and I think that with what you know combined with what I know, you know, I know, David—

Message erased. Next new message. From, phone number two three four, seven three two, seven eight four two. Received, February fourth at ten-twenty-five a.m.

Please come see me. I can't stay here wondering. I know you're sitting somewhere wondering what's going on. We have that in common. I can't see clients. I can't see them without seeing her. She's everywhere.

Message erased. First saved message. From, phone number three three zero, eight four five, three four three three. Received, October fifteenth at eleven-eleven a.m.

Hey. Please wash and prep the vegetables before I get home. We're in a hurry. Sorry. See you.

Saved. There are no more messages. Main menu. Listen, one. Send, two. Personal options, three. Call, eight. Exit, star.

First saved message. From, phone number three three zero, eight four five, three four three three. Received, October fifteenth at eleven-eleven a.m.

Hey. Please wash and prep the vegetables before I get home. We're in a hurry. Sorry. See you.

Saved. There are no more messages. Main menu. Listen, one. Send, two. Personal options, three. Call, eight. Exit, star.

First saved message. From, phone number three three zero, eight four five, three four three three. Received, October fifteenth at eleven-eleven a.m.

Hey. Please wash and prep the vegetables before I get home. We're in a hurry. Sorry. See you.

Saved. There are no more messages. Main menu. Listen, one. Send, two. Personal options, three. Call, eight. Exit, star. To indicate your choice, press the number of the option you wish to select. Whenever you need more information about the options, press zero for help. You can interrupt these instructions at any time by pressing a key to make your selection.

68

AN EARLY THAW CAME. Brown birds alighted on branches and took in the scene. Ice gave way to slush, which chilled the sewer grates as it slipped through and iced again in the old dead leaves hidden underneath. A pregnant deer walked uncertainly through the yard, frowned in a way a deer frowns, and walked up the road. The world uncovered itself. Children who had been born in winter saw the melting world for the first time, and they were wary.

David took a long walk around the neighborhood. His neighbors were out shoveling rotten leaves. Everyone was still in their winter gear but seemed more optimistic about things.

One of the houses that had been up for sale all winter had been quietly bought. It was different from the others, single story, and set back from the road, taking advantage of the deep lot. There were five workers on the roof when David walked by. It was hard to see what they were doing and he stood at the end of the driveway, watching. Three of the workers slopped sealant from buckets while the other two spread it thin. The sun glinted off their long rakes.

There was a woman at the front window. David had not immediately seen her, because she was as large as the window itself, which seemed like an illusion with the house set back so far. She had looked like a curtain in the window, wearing a dark dress or a robe. If he were closer, he could more clearly see the expression on her face.

Before he could register that the woman had Franny's build and height, a man opened the front door and emerged on the front step, and David saw that it was the man from the bus stop a month earlier, or three months, his direct copy, the same glasses and jacket and sneakers and stride. He held his hand up to shade his eyes from the sun, and David realized he was also holding his own hand in the same way. He lifted his other hand and waved once. A nerve ending fluttered over his lower left rib. He thought of the time he and Franny stayed in a cabin in the woods and walked until they found a pond and looked at it, not holding hands or even standing near each other, so a stranger approaching from the trail would see two additional strangers, three strangers total meeting at a pond and looking into it.

The man waved back, and the woman was gone from the window. The man walked forward and David felt himself walking back as if pushed, as if the world's balance now required that the two men remain a precise distance apart. The man had opened his mouth and was saying something, gesturing; David was gesturing behind himself toward the road, and with no small effort he turned away from the man and walked briskly and then jogged and ran, slipping on the slush and startling another deer that had been prodding leaves with its snout, sending the deer bounding into the woods, ash trees falling away by the time David reached the road and kept on running, the wind's chill mixing with the sun on his face and in his eyes.

69

AILEEN PUSHED the metal extractor into the face of one of her younger clients. The woman's skin had been so clogged that she seemed to have pinpoint black freckles. Still, as she worked under the examination light, Aileen marveled at the smooth skin in the usual trouble spots, the calming sense of a flawless palette between the eyes. She directed the steam wand at the girl's face and readied her tools while the pores bloomed.

Her extractor resembled a dentist's device, which is to say it resembled a torture device. The sharp edge on one side was designed to slacken the skin so that the scoop on the other side could coax out the offending oil plug. With the steam wand, Aileen didn't often need to use the sharp side on young skin. She would simply press the scoop gently and collect the emerging waste. The skin of older women tended to be more set in its ways.

She began the process of extracting the pores, wiping the waste onto a towel beside her. Her client was a regular, and Aileen knew that she had one extraction point to save for last. The woman kept a blackhead tucked at the corner of her lip, cradled by a protective layer of skin that fed and supported it.

The skin folded over the concealed blackhead and hid it. The woman was largely ashamed of her skin's texture and quality, as she well should be, but she had a strange pride in the single blackhead. Instead of treating it with the acids Aileen prescribed, the woman layered the area with oil-based makeup, nourishing it, growing it like a seedpod covered by a warm layer of earth. When Aileen birthed it into her metal scoop, the woman sighed with the effort and release of it. Aileen brushed the lancet blade of her extractor over the edge of the woman's lip with a surgeon's precise motion. The woman's lip twitched at the housefly feeling of the blade caressing her vellus hair.

Aileen walked the woman to the front desk and found David standing there. The skin on his face was dull and curled up red under his nose and at the corners of his mouth. She thought of the collected years of dead and dying bacteria on the man's face at that moment.

"We need to have a conversation," he said.

"Come on back. I'll give you a freebie."

She hadn't cleaned the room after the previous client. David climbed onto the reclined chair without removing his boots. Aileen switched on the light, and his face gleamed with clotted oil. He tipped his head back like an obedient child when she applied cleanser with a cotton round. He murmured his approval. "Franny did this at night sometimes," he said.

She looked at the cotton round coming up black and brown in the soft light. "Your skin is filthy."

"She took care of me."

Aileen spread an acid enzyme mask on his face using a brush. He winced, and she knew the pain he felt. "So talk," she said.

"I think she's been living in a house down the street," he said. "There is a house that looks like ours, and a man lives there. It's possible she has been living there."

She pointed the jet of air from a steam machine toward his forehead, which seemed to be the worst offender in terms of congealed cells. She became distinctly aware of his clothes. They were soiled to the point where the filth of his body had its own texture. She lowered her lips to his ear, where the hair curled in long ringlets and tucked over the tips of his earlobes. "I see her everywhere," she said.

"My face stings."

"Just a few more minutes."

She heard another noise over the hiss of the steam machine and realized it was David sighing through his nose. He sighed until the air seemed to leave his body completely, and then he was still for a moment, and then he breathed in again, taking the moist, warm air into his body. "I don't think she ever left," he said.

"I saw her on the bus," Aileen said. "I saw her walking. I thought she had decided to take a break from our friendship. I called after her, but she didn't turn around. Her body shifted five degrees to the left. I saw her walking up a side street three blocks from where we usually walk. She stood at a wall at the end of the street and pressed it as if to move it." Her eyes were wild. "She didn't turn around when I called."

Without opening his eyes, David reached both hands up and grasped Aileen's face. He pulled her toward him and kissed her, his mouth so wide that it seemed more like his mouth was in a competition with hers, his tongue a wall on her lips, spackling their gloss, removing her lipstick and absorbing it. The acid mess on his face smeared her cheeks and immediately melted the first two layers of her makeup through the foundation, leaching the color off her face. She pressed her face down with the idea of crushing him and kissed his tongue and teeth, sucking the fluids there, tasting bitter coffee and mouthwash, internalizing his mouth, pressing her face harder and licking the strangely flat surface of his back teeth, wishing for a moment that she could take his teeth in her mouth and chew on them, feel the foreign against familiar, his teeth embedding in her cheeks like cloves in an orange. She kicked back her rolling chair and moved to the center of the reclined treatment chair without separating from his mouth. She unbuttoned David's pants, straddled the chair, tugged her underwear to the side under her skirt with her thumb. It was old underwear, she remembered while pulling him out of his pants, the kind that was once an optimistic deep purple and had since bleached out, slackening elastic at the edges, like webbing between the fingers of the retired women who came in for bleaching and injectables, their hands puddled together on bloated bellies, smiling into the light. He was almost completely soft, but she stuffed him into her with sticky fingers. He groaned, and instinct bucked his hips. The acid that had been on her hands burned their genitals. They were still kissing, eating bitter enzyme. She spit onto his shirt. Her eyes stung. He tried to shift their position but couldn't move in the small chair. He slipped out of her and she piled him back in, squeezed his body between her legs, held him completely still, digging her nails into his stomach. One of them was crying. She kissed his neck and left a trail of slime. When she bit him he cried out and looked up at her for the first time, his eyes red and swollen nearly shut.

She climbed off and left the room without comment. He lay on the table waiting for her to come back, but she didn't. After he was sure she wouldn't come back, he buttoned his pants and stood.

He couldn't find her in the lobby or at any of the hair stations. One of the girls told him that Aileen had gone home early for the day. "She's not here," the girl said, "right hand to God." She was twisting and pulling at the twin lumps of fat above her hips, pinching her body like an unbaked loaf.

DAVID didn't like going into the backyard. Stickers burred into his ankle hair. Franny had always done the work of clearing brush and splitting fire logs, and there were times when she vanished out into one of the two acres beyond and returned with a handful of berries or a flattened soda can. Sometimes she found slivers of stone that she thought were arrowheads, though it seemed as if she had never seen an actual arrowhead. The rocks she brought in had been smoothed by time. She kept them in a bowl on the bathroom counter.

Out back, the earth looked differently trampled. A gum wrapper fluttered in a spiny bush, silver paper shivering against the red berries. He thought of what Aileen had said about all the people who had died in the history of that place, after the spiny bush had grown there but, more important, before the bush and the stream beside it and the house and the old farmer's fence made of barbed wire and splintered posts that rotted lower every year. David had been meaning to remove the old fence. He had not gotten around to it. Before the fence and the ash trees, or when there were different trees, or perhaps when it was all underwater, when strange and ordinary aquatic creatures floated and consumed one another and left their remains buried under five to ten feet of silt that hardened into stone and was covered with pieces of flint and slate, which his wife mistook for arrowheads but were wholly unremarkable rocks after all.

On the far side of the farmer's fence, he found a frozen pear and beside it a sock trampled into the ground. It was one of David's gym socks, mealy from the earth that had been pushed into it, half hidden under a root. He bent to pick the sock up and found that it was folded around its mate. He used the toe of his shoe to unearth them and found another pair nestled alongside. Crouching down, he found another pair underneath, black dress socks next to a larger pink-striped variety. A sandwich bag stuffed full of hosiery lay underneath and under that, a pair of insulating socks David had been missing for years. He dug away at the top layer of earth, thinking about stopping and going to the garage for a shovel but certain that if he returned, the socks would be gone, hundreds of them, the collected effort of many years. There were his father's trouser socks with their gold-stitched toes. He found a shoebox underneath a stratum of unpaired single socks. Moisture and age had worn away the box's distinguishing marks. There was some difficulty in clearing it from the frozen earth, which hardly yielded against his digging gloved hands. He wedged the tips of his fingers against the side of the box and then got a grip on the side of it and pulled it out. The box had been laid over three pairs of small faded pink lace socks. They looked like mice huddled together. He could hold all three pairs in the palm of his hand.

David put the baby socks in his pocket and laid the shoebox beside the shallow trench. In it he found the pair of woolen socks he had bought Franny for one of their anniversaries, the anniversary when one buys wool. She had bought him a leatherbound desk set for his office at home, with a leather tray for papers and a pencil holder and a protective desk cover and a small file cabinet that also was somehow leather, the stitches so fine he could barely see them. He had put it at the reception desk at work, and the receptionist said she felt like she was less of a receptionist and more of an executive secretary, so fine was the leatherwork. The receptionist's demeanor improved over the phone, and patients seemed more relaxed when they got to the chair. Franny's gift to him had been the best gift he had ever received, and in return he handed her a pair of socks, because he was confused, and he thought it was to be the anniversary when one buys wool. It was a gift he had been ashamed of, but she wore the socks faithfully for years. She washed them carefully in the sink and wore them for anniversaries in the years following, until one year when she did not wear them, and David felt a secret sense of relief and didn't mention it out of fear that she would apologize and bring them out. He had forgotten about them. But there they were, alone in the box. They were a speckled gray and black with points of white. He thought of her burying them. If she had been sitting next to him at that moment, he would say a great many things, but he was alone. There was a page in the sock, but he was tired of knowing how to read, so he opened his mouth and inserted the page. The paper he had packed into his teeth rolled up and allowed for the new intrusion. His jaw popped and widened farther. The page was warm on his teeth and felt natural against his tongue. His lips cracked and bled into it, but he kept opening his mouth wider, pushing it toward the back of his throat, twisting the paper to corkscrew it in farther, breathing hard through his nose as it reached the back of his throat, pushed against his soft palate, caressed his palatine uvula. He gagged and clenched his teeth, and the page compacted and became a part of him, there in his mouth.

71

THE SUGAR CEREAL was not in the break-room cabinet nor under the sink. It was not in the reception desk. It was not in the large lower desk drawer belonging to an officer who hoarded sweets. It was not in Chico's office and it was not in the paper towel dispenser in the bathroom. It was not in his aunt's bag of clothes, folded beside her. The boy had made a detailed list of where the sugar cereal might be and had crossed off possible options. Behind one of the chairs in the reception area, check. Tucked within the fire extinguisher's glass case, check. He checked the break room's refrigerator and freezer, opening all drawers, moving aside forgotten baggies of spoiled sandwiches and frozen-over potpies, looking for the slightest clue. He attached the list to a clipboard, which he carried under his arm.

His aunt was waiting for him in the reception area. She had found a word search among the scattered newspapers and smoothed the sheet of newspaper over her knee, looking up every so often to find the boy.

He stood on the chair beside her, unscrewing the light switch with a small screwdriver. "There's one," said the boy, leaning down to point at the page.

Shelly circled the word "snow." "The sugar cereal is not going to be behind the light switch."

"It's unlikely," he said, popping the screws out of the switch plate and into his hand. He tried to remove the plate but couldn't catch the width of it in his small hand and dropped the screwdriver to get a better grip. "I'm taking this case past likelihood and moving straight into possibility." Using his fingernails, he pried the plate off and peered into the darkness around the device.

"Are you sure you didn't eat the sugar cereal?"

He replaced the switch plate, picked a screw out of his palm, and threaded it into place. He picked up the small screwdriver and fit it into its notch and tightened it. The screwdriver had come from Shelly's glasses-repair kit, which she kept in her purse.

"Or probably someone else ate it?"

Her nephew dropped to a kneeling position on the chair and slowly placed one foot on the floor and then the other, with the kind of care a much smaller child would employ. She held her bag of clothes to the side in case he fell toward them. He had always been a careful boy.

"We have a high standard of moral conduct around here," the boy said. "The ladies and gentlemen of this office are charged with upholding the law, as I'm sure you're aware. Nobody is going to knowingly come into this office and eat sugar cereal that doesn't belong to them." He had picked up his clipboard again.

Shelly patted the chair next to her and he frowned but clambered up again, grasping the chair's back rail and turning to sit beside her.

She put her arm around his shoulders and hugged him to her. "It doesn't really matter where the sugar cereal is, does it?"

"Sure it does. If someone hid it, finding where it's hidden will help me know who did it. If someone ate it, there will be evidence, and I'll find it, and then something can be done. I should check the wastebins." He scanned the items on his clipboard list and started to slide off the chair when Shelly tightened the grip on his shoulder.

"But if you think about it," she said, "it doesn't really matter."

The boy was silent, staring at his clipboard.

Shelly released his shoulder and circled another word, "fence." "Remember what we learned about what happens to the cereal, and the candy in the cereal, and all of us?" she asked.

The boy used his careful handwriting to write "leaves" on the page, and then crossed it out just as carefully. "It's out there somewhere," he said to the page.

"That's right," Shelly said. "Now it's time to go and have some dinner."

She stood and hefted him off the chair and onto his feet. He unlocked the receptionist's desk drawer and put the clipboard inside. The key to the desk was on its own ring, which he attached to a lanyard around his neck and tucked under his shirt. The key was cold on his stomach, then it was warm, and then he couldn't feel it at all. He followed his aunt out of the office.

72

THE LAUNDRY BASKET had been too awkward to carry up the hill. Shelly left it at the bus stop and bundled the clothes in a towel to haul on her back. She did not look at the address written on her hand, because she had heard it would be the only house on the street with boarded windows. She walked to the garage and knocked on the open door.

"Knock-knock," Shelly said.

A woman raised her hand from her desk. "The detective said you'd stop by," she said. "Let me move my papers."

"Don't go to any trouble for me," Shelly said, widening the door with her shoulder. She entered the room and laid her bundle on a chair in front of the desk. Wasps swarmed and dotted the towel.

The woman was gathering folders from where they lay scattered atop an old white-lacquered washing machine. "Don't mind them," she said.

The wasps were chaining themselves together to form a necklace around Shelly's neck. She resisted the urge to lift her hand. "I thought a change of scenery was in order," Shelly said.

The other woman lifted folders to her chest and hefted them off the washer. She spread the papers out on the countertop and sifted through them. "I need to organize my life," she said.

"Thank you for making room," Shelly said. She waved her hands over the towel, and the wasps took flight. Her living necklace dissipated. One landed on her hand and made a delicate path toward her fingertips. Shelly stood quietly and allowed the movement, which felt like a caress over the tiny hairs along her mid-digits.

The woman was watching. "Wasps don't have hairs on their legs that capture pollen like bees do. They used to eat meat."

The wasp walked across Shelly's fingertips. She brought her hand closer to her face to see the tiny claws at the ends of the wasp's feet. "There's nothing wrong with you," she said to the wasp.

"They still have the bodies of predators."

Shelly moved her hand with the wasp toward the washing machine, reaching into her pocket for a quarter with the other. She placed the quarter next to the insect, holding her wasp hand level. The wasp regarded the quarter and touched it with a quivering mandible, then released Shelly's hand and headed for the roof. Shelly put the quarter down and picked up the laundry. "Thank you for making room for me," she said to the ceiling. The room's rafters swelled with movement.

"No problem. It's nice to have company," the woman said, unwrapping a stick of gum. She had stacked her folders and opened a book at her desk, though it was clear she wasn't reading it. She put the gum in her mouth and moved her fingers across the page as if the words were printed on ridges. "Do you know about 'you'?" she asked.

Shelly thought about it. "About as much as could be expected," she said. "I wouldn't say I know the whole depth and breadth."

"More devastation has been linked to 'you' than anything else. The research is conclusive. I've researched the full canon. Since it was 'thou.' We're talking over six hundred years of devastation. Heartbreak. Accusation. And worst, worst? False promise." She leaned back in her chair and tapped a stack of books rising up from the floor, reaching above her elbow. "A lifetime of plans, dissolved. Each of them linked to 'you.' Tied there in the history of the world."

Shelly balanced the clothes on her hip. "If it wasn't me, it would be you."

"It is 'you.'" The woman worked her gum like a cud. "Can you imagine the history of the world without 'you'?"

"I appreciate you saying that," Shelly said, opening the washer lid. She ran her hand around the interior of the machine to pull out the forgotten tissues. At the bottom of the tub, she touched a ribbon, satin against her hand. The ribbon was stuck partially under the lower rim of the agitator. She tugged at it and worked her hand under the plastic rim. It had gone through a cycle or two and was wrapped around the agitator. Leaving it there would immobilize the agitator, leading to a highly imperfect wash. Shelly pushed the agitator to one side and pulled on the ribbon in the opposite direction. She felt the ribbon sliding and tearing against the plastic piece, and then it was free, and her hand came back holding the ribbon looped around two gold wedding bands and knotted tight. She held the rings close to her eye. The ribbon was pale pink and lined with stitched eyelets. It looked like the kind of ribbon that would be woven through a baby's bonnet. She put one of the rings between her teeth and made an impression in the gold.

"What is it?" Marie asked.

Shelly held the rings up. "History of the world," she said.

73

DAVID'S MOTHER fumbled with the foil crimping over the carton of juice. She tried to pinch it between her thumb and forefinger, but the thin tab of foil and her blindness worked together to elude her. She scratched at the foil-crimped lid, as if to puncture it, but succeeded only in flattening some of the minor perforations of metal, bowing it in. David reached for her hands to help but she pulled them back, protecting the juice with her forearm. The attendant standing at the corner of the room already knew not to go to the trouble of an advance and assist.

"There was a court case in one of the southern states years ago," she said, "twenty years ago. The only witness to the act in question was a five-year-old child, a boy. Without question he had witnessed the act. His mother's lawyer led him to the stand, and the judge asked the boy what color the lawyer's tie was. The boy said it was blue, and the judge said, no, that tie is red. The boy was confused and said it was blue and the judge said that the tie was red and the boy was very bad if he thought it was blue."

"What color was the tie?"

"Yellow, that's the thing. There's an interesting tale about the minds of children." She had run a divot in the foil with her fingernail, and she went back to trying to grasp the edge with her thumb and forefinger.

"They searched the house," David said.

She squeezed the plastic juice carton until one section of the foil, weakened from the struggle, lifted from the corner. A dribble of juice leaked into her hand, and she laughed and put her finger into her mouth. "Did they find her?" she asked.

"Franny?"

Bright drops of juice spilled onto the table, and she took her finger from her mouth, bent her head to the table, and held her lips to the drops. She pressed her tongue to the table and slurped the juice. "Your sister," she said into the table, smacking her lips as if she tasted a delicious dish. "Did they find your sister?"

"That's over, Mom."

His mother had stopped smacking her lips. She turned her head slightly and rested her left cheek on the wet print her tongue had left. "Things were never quite right," she said. "It was my fault, with your sister. The doctors gave me pills and I took them."

"You don't need to say that."

"Your father and I loved you and we loved your sister, but things were never quite right with her. It was my fault."

David had a vision of his mother delivering a speech face-down on the table. The speech would be about drug use, and she could tour the state offering it to middle school students. Each school would provide a chair, a table, and a microphone that had a broad enough range of motion to bend and nearly touch the woman's lips, which now repeated the mouth shapes required to create the words "your" and "sister" without sound. On cue with visiting hours ending, the woman in the corner advanced to hook her heavy arms under David's mother's arm-pits, pulling her gently back into her wheelchair with care, the attendant's eyes blankly suggesting she had done this many times before with many other confused mothers who had all ultimately tried their best to form a family.

At the bus stop outside, David noticed how dry and clean the air felt. The snow had melted, and the landscape featured blooming buds. He found, carved into the bench:

SORRY ABOUT ALL THIS.

74

MARIE HEARD THE CARS PULL UP and saw the officers organize. "The police are here," she said, watching from her spot at the garage door. The other woman was still stooped over her laundry, folding and unfolding, as she had for the past thirty minutes. The stack of folded clothes was on the floor, which Marie had not ever swept and which was thick with wasp bodies and the webs of spiders. Fifty years of motor oil and dryer lint had layered underneath the bodies. Marie tried to imagine the poured-concrete floor without the mired gunk but could think only of chemicals she might pour onto the floor to try to cut it. An acid, perhaps combined with a few passes from a power washer, though it would require her to move her papers. The thought of all her papers outside in boxes filled her with sadness. The woman had been folding a striped polo shirt for ten minutes and was at that moment tucking the fabric of the sleeves behind the trunk with her fingertips. She leaned forward to examine her angle of attack on the fold. Stooped like that, she looked like a scientist examining a specimen.

"Police are here," Marie said.

"I'm sure they've got a good reason," said the woman.

Marie looked back out the door and saw that they were headed toward the house. Chico was among them.

"I should let them in," Marie said.

"That sounds helpful of you."

Marie found the keys in the desk drawer and headed for the house. "Helpful of you," she said to herself as she walked.

75

ON APRIL 11, I was on the North Side when I received
a call to assist a detective with a search warrant order. I arrived
on the scene to find Detective Chico with Officers Riley and
Hanson on the scene. Officer Marks arrived shortly after I did.
The home had boards over the windows and seemed abandoned. Detective Chico knocked on the door. There was no
response. The process was repeated, and Detective Chico noted
that he was concerned for the safety of parties inside the home.
Due to departmental lack of funds, a battering ram had not
been purchased. Officers Riley and Hanson began to consider
entering via the window. At this time, a woman arrived on the
scene with a key that unlocked the door. There were no lights
on in the house, and the officers deployed their flashlights.
There was a strong smell of urine, which the officers noticed
and remarked upon. There was broken glass on the kitchen
counter. Officer Marks took photographs of each room. The
stairs to the basement were deemed impassable by the officers
due to a buildup of discarded books, print media, and containers filled with the above, and Detective Chico made a note to

call in a secondary crew for further search if necessary. Their flashlights swept the room. The team ascended the stairs and searched the master bedroom, at which point the detective and officers found a dark room full of items such as newspapers, magazines, greeting cards, books without book covers, blank computer paper, empty cardboard boxes, tissue paper, wood shavings, Post-it notes, index cards, receipts, and other materials. On the bed, one individual was found and deemed unresponsive. The individual was positively identified by Detective Chico as David B███. When officers neared, they found that the man was agitated, and his breathing had been hindered. An urn was opened by his side, and it appeared that he had spread its enclosed contents over his body. Paramedics were called. The officers attempted to help Mr. B███ remove some of the items from his mouth or pull them from his hands, but he refused their assistance. When they reached for his mouth, he moved his face to the side and became agitated. He would not release the paper in his hands, and he became aggressive, swinging his arms from his position on the bed. Two of the officers caught his arms and held him until the paramedics arrived. Mr. B███ was weeping throughout and making a groaning noise during this time. Paramedics arrived and additionally aided in restraining him. When he was restrained, it was revealed that he had been holding in his mouth a balled-up page upon which words were typed. Detective Chico found the page and documented its contents while paramedics attended to Mr. B███.

76.

PAPER ~~SAILBOAT~~ ON A STILL LAKE MY DEAR CARRY IT AWAY
CARRY IT ~~HURRY~~ MY DEER IN THE WOODS, I'M ~~LOST~~, I
FOUND A NOTE WITH YOUR NAME / I FOUND A PLATE ON
THE WATER, A PAPER PLATE ON A STILL LAKE THIS DRAINED
~~AORTA~~ FEELS THERE'S NO BRUISE THIS UNBLUSHED BLEM-
ISH THIS MISTAKE THAT ~~ORBITS~~ MY BODY MY LOVE DO
YOU BELIEVE THE FLOATING ALTAR FINDS A DRAWN PATH,
FUTURES ~~LUSHLY~~ DESCRIBED WITH A PRACTICED HAND /
MY DEAR DARLING HAVE YOU EVER BEEN A LAMB HAVE
YOU EVER IN A MOMENT FELT THE NEED TO ~~ABHOR~~ THE
EARTH FOR IT COMPACTS INTO A NUT WITH EVERY FAIL-
ING FOOTFALL AND EACH MIND DIES ~~SOLITARY~~ RE-
MEMBER THE TIME WE REMEMBERED, REMEMBER THE
STEAMING CRACK IN THE EARTH, REMEMBER ~~LUST~~ AND IF
YOU DO, REMIND ME / REMEMBER THE ~~ALTARS~~ ALL IN
WHITE, YOUR HANDS PRESS THE WALL SEARCHING YOUR
HANDS OH HEAVENS DO YOU THINK THAT'S OUT THERE
DO YOU REMEMBER THE WAY A SWEET MEAT LOOKS
AFTER A GOOD ~~BROIL~~ WHAT'S IN A FOOT IN THE EARTH

WHAT'S PUTTING DOWN ROOTS SWEET ~~YOUTHS~~ WHAT'S
IN A NAME BUT STICKS AND BRANCHES / AFFIX YOUR BIL-
LOW AND ~~SAIL~~ MY LOVE, PUSH FROM THE SHORE, YOUR
FEET BARE AS A ~~SATYR~~ YOUR FEET UNSHOD, I DO LOVE A
GOOD RIDDLE MY LOVE AND YOU WERE THE BEST, ~~BLOT~~
YOUR EYES, TAKE MY TISSUE, I HAVE ANOTHER, I HAVE AN-
OTHER ~~HOUR~~ BEFORE YOU FIND ME / OH DEAR SORRY
ABOUT THE ~~BLOAT~~ SORRY ABOUT THE AFFECTED ~~AIRS~~ IN
THE END WE'RE ALL HOLDING VEILS WALKING IN A LINE
WE'RE ~~HOLY~~ VEILS WALKING IN A LINE OF ANTS DO YOU
REMEMBER WHEN THE ~~RUST~~ WAS SO HIGH AROUND OUR
EYES, WE THOUGHT WE WOULD BE WET FOREVER / A PA-
PER ~~BOATS~~ ON A STILL LAKE, FLOATING SILENT DOWN
THE ~~RILL~~, CATCHING SWEETLY ON SHINING PEBBLE,
FLIGHT OF ~~RAYS~~ SHINES THE WATER, MAKE THE MISTAKE
~~THOU~~ MAKE THE MISTAKE THUS THAT THESE DAYS WILL
NEVER EVER, THESE DAYS WILL NEVER / A LONG TIME AGO
WHEN I WAS A GIRL AND WE WERE ALL ONCE GIRLS SAYS
SCIENCE, LOOK IT UP, IN THE LONG TIME AGO WHEN I WAS
ALL ONCE GIRLS IN THE FOREST ONCE I MEAN TO SAY I
FOUND AN ~~ALTAR~~ THERE IN THE WOODS, A BRANCH COV-
ERING LEFT CAREFULLY, I LOOKED LEFT AND RIGHT AND
THEN TUCKED IT BACK AND FOUND A WASHED PAN OF
BRICKS AND STONE, OBJECTS ARRANGED AND IN THE
CENTER A ~~BOLUS~~ OF SWEET SKULL AND TISSUE, AN OWL
SAVING A FINE CHEW FOR LATER, THE PERISHED CREA-
TURE PRESENTS ITS ~~HISTORY~~ THERE TO FIND OR NOT
FIND, FOR US TO THINK OR NOT THINK THAT SOMEDAY WE
MIGHT BE SUCH / I SPENT THE DAY INVENTING ~~ABATTOIRS~~
FOR INDIVIDUALS WHO ARE TECHNICALLY WELL BUT

JUST A LITTLE TIRED OF WAITING TO SEE WHAT'S NEXT, DO YOU KNOW WHAT I MEAN DO YOU KNOW ~~HOLY~~ WAYS TO LOOK AT A BOAT, ANYTHING GAINS SIGNIFICANCE WHEN YOU PUT IT ON AN ALTAR, THAT'S THE THING ABOUT ALTARS, ABOUT THINGS, EVEN A ~~SLUR~~ SPARKLES WELL ENOUGH THAT YOUR OWN MOTHER COULD PICK IT UP AND HOLD IT IN HER HANDS, YOUR DEER MOTHER / OH HEAVENS DID I ALREADY APOLOGIZE FOR THE ~~BLOAT~~ DID I ALREADY COMB YOUR ~~HAIR~~ OH MY SWEET DEAR, WE NEVER DID ~~TRY~~ TO HAVE OUR TIME DID WE, OUR ~~SOULS~~ WAVE FROM ACROSS THE WATER, THE WAVELESS WATER, BETWEEN US A PAPER BOAT FLOATS BY WHICH I MEAN TO SAY, BY WHICH I STILL MEAN, BY WHICH A STILL LAKE /

"SOMETHING has happened."

They had eaten breakfast together that morning, like any morning, every morning. She ate like a large, hungry bird. Mostly seeds. She looked out the window. On the mornings he asked her what she was looking at, she said she was looking at the world.

It was snowing. The snow fell harder than it had fallen all year, and steady enough to create drifts in the ash trees, where snow piled on nests and old leaves, inside of which animals burrowed, their eyes dimmed for the necessity of survival. "You've been tromping berries."

The berries behind the house were speckled against the snow. She had tried to eat one of the berries once. It was bitter. "It's blood. Could you call for help?" He thought of her eyes, an animal's dark eyes. Later, when the officers swept the scene, they shook the snow from the berry bushes and examined the berries as evidence. Snow had fallen over her tracks from the fence.

"Of course. What's the problem?" An expanse of time viewed from a distance, a horizon. He could live in the place where he saw her eyes. It was simple to live in a place.

Her body swayed, her feet bare. "God, damn it." The workers who would come to clean the stairwell did not think about the origin of the stains to which they applied enzyme cleaner. One added up the number of cleanings required to repair the heater in his car. Another tried to remember if cleaning products had been ordered for the week. A third thought about his girlfriend's hair on a pillow that morning, soft like a baby's.

"What did you do? What happened?" That morning, she spooned the sugar into her cup of coffee and returned the bag to the pantry. She walked to the table and sat beside him. These things were as ordinary as ordinary. Missing them would feel the same as missing a chair that was not particularly comfortable or uncomfortable. Like missing a dinner plate, a door's frame.

The course of events stood in a silent line, serving as sentries for the individuals who moved helpless among them. "Could you call the fire department?" Anything seemed possible, but only one thing was possible. "You don't need to call anyone. Forget about it. I love you."

"What did you get into?" The mess had frozen to her ankles, her feet, her toes, but she was thawing, a river of bright blood carving through. Her body warming to the indoors would be the end of her, but the idea of coming inside would have been too natural to ignore, even if she had an awareness of the danger, which she had not.

Her body was so cold against his. He reached for her, put his arms around her, warmed her. He put the warmth of his hands onto her wet feet until his hands were cold, and then he warmed his hands on his own neck, his stomach under his flannel pajamas, his armpits, and then laid his hands on her again, rubbing, warming without knowing that he was stimulating the arterial wound. "That's your problem." Her body moved beyond ache to something else. She felt like a bird in a nest. Time passed like a snowdrift.

"Doc," he said. "You gotta understand." He tried to move her legs into his lap, but she waved him off, laughing. Her laugh stopped his motion and he looked at her. His face was a panel. She felt a desire to touch her nose to his nose, such a pleasurable desire, and not acting on it made it a secret, which made it even more of a pleasure. He watched her. She was too tired then to express the desire aloud, and the secret became even more perfect. It became the most perfect secret she had ever experienced, as close as she was to him at that moment. Her heart pounded with pleasure. It seemed possible to express anything by looking at him, and so she looked, the energy leaving her feet and hands and filling her eyes. Her mouth slackened as she directed every electric impulse of energy into her eyes, which watched him and twitched slightly, scanning his eyes, imparting every truth with perfect clarity. She leaned against the stairwell, smiling, looking at him even when her eyes lost their energy and their light faded.

Her body swelled and stilled. There would be a moment when she would breathe for the last time. An exhalation. There would be that moment for him as well, for all, but it was her moment at that moment, her prize of air, her still lake, her sweet boat floating away away, her body warping wood, swale and heavy, a sinking thing. He sat beside her, a helpless observer, his only power in witness, some bleak ability to watch and record the event in his own brain, which sent the order to his lungs to breathe with her while she still breathed, channels rising, sparks of interior electrical connection fading with the mind's fool hope that it could create some kind of measurable response, to provide some worth or warmth. Her body beside his, swell and still. He thought of her still. He thought of holding her absolutely still. He loved, he loved her. He loved her, still.

Acknowledgments

Thanks are owed to Emily Bell, Justin Boyle, Claudia Ballard, Maxine Bartow, Lisa Silverman, and Debra Helfand for their attention and care in the production of this book. Thanks also to Featherproof Books and Fiction Collective Two, Ron Carlson, Tom Grimes, Mike McNally, Debra Monroe, and my family.